"Parker, I can go, if you don't need me here."

"No, please. You're the first date I've had since—"

"This isn't a date."

"No," Parker sighed. "It isn't, but I'd like to take you out. A movie, maybe. Dinner?"

"I don't know." Izzy sat at the scratched, wooden table. "Parker, can I ask you something?"

"Anything."

"What do you think about God?"

Parker turned and cracked eggs into a skillet. The sound of popping and sizzling barely dented a silence so tangible it could almost be touched. "I don't think about Him."

Could Parker Strickland be desperate enough to take his own life? Isobelle de la Rosa wondered, after reading the journal he'd mistakenly returned to the library. It hadn't been long since the handsome fireman had lost his wife, but would depression cause him to end his own existence?

As Parker pushed aside all her efforts to help, the librarian's concern deepened. Did none of the townspeople see his pain? If so, why would so many plot to turn them into a couple?

PAMELA KAYE TRACY decided to be an author in second grade. When she grew up, God also put her in charge of a third-grade classroom (by day) and added a college reading class (by night). When not teaching, Pamela spends her time writing, sewing, reading, and staying active at her church. She makes her home in Arizona. She is owned by a huge black and white cat. *It Only Takes a Spark* is her first published novel.

It Only Takes a Spark

Pamela Kaye Tracy

Heartsong Presents

To my parents:
Albert H. Tracy and Rosemary A. Tracy (1927-1992)
When I said I wanted to sing, they listened.
When I said I wanted to draw, they provided pencils.
When I said I wanted to write, they gave me paper,
and through it all they gave me love.

And to my aunt and uncle:
Arnold Wilfong and Catherine Wilfong (1915-1993)
Every child needs cheerleaders. You were mine.

A note from the author:
*I love to hear from my readers! You may correspond with me
by writing:*   **Pamela Kaye Tracy**
Author Relations
PO Box 719
Uhrichsville, OH 44683

ISBN 1-57748-624-2

IT ONLY TAKES A SPARK

All of the characters and events in this book are fictitious. Any
resemblance to actual persons, living or dead, or to actual events
is purely coincidental.

Cover illustration by Adam Wallenta.

PRINTED IN THE U.S.A.

"I'll be there in four more months." Isobelle de la Rosa expertly propped the phone between her ear and shoulder while propping her feet on her boss's desk and twirling a strand of black hair around her finger. "Mom's doing much better, and Carole's baby is due any day now."

Carole Martin waddled into the office, smiled as if she knew a secret, and set a stack of books on the large table that took up most of the office's space. Pressing a hand to the small of her back, she waited for Izzy to finish talking.

"I gotta go," Izzy sang into the phone, winking at Carole. "You know how my boss is."

"Was that Connie?" Carole put one hand on the table for balance and knocked a bulging folder to the floor.

"Yes." Izzy jumped up, came around the desk, and bent to retrieve the papers littered across the carpet. She carefully returned them to the stacks of things to do already towering on the head librarian's desk and scolded, "You're in your eighth month. You should be sitting down."

"There's too much to do." Carole frowned at the phone as if it had committed a crime. "If you're really going back to Phoenix come January, I've got to train the new girl, learn the computer system, and at least finish converting some of the card catalogue entries onto disc. All that and have a baby, too." Carole glanced at a photograph on her desk. Her husband, robust and graying, posed with a politician's smile. Their two college-age children flanked him. Carole grinned and shook her head. "Pregnant at forty-five, what was I thinking? Oh, well, Jake says it will keep us young at heart. Izzy, I can't locate any of Erma Bombeck's books on the computer. Will you come out and initiate a search for me?"

Carole left the room. Izzy said a quick prayer. She'd tried to see to it that her boss didn't spend much time on her feet. Carole had gotten slower with each pound gained, until her blossoming body mainly took up residence behind the check-out counter and dealt with patrons. That left Izzy to do everything else. Carole's desk had lately become Izzy's. The stress of dealing with learning the new computer system, bar coding the hundreds of books, convincing seasoned patrons about the wonders of the electronic age, and responding to the newspaper's editorials about censorship inspired Carole to turn more of the duties over to Izzy. The amount of work piling up on the desk testified a real need for organization.

Glancing at the calendar, Izzy tabulated how long she'd worked at Mayhill Library. One year, six months.

Izzy brushed a quick hand through her long hair and again reminded herself that she certainly didn't fit the stereotype for a small-town librarian. Yet, Carole seemed to approve of Izzy's charge-ahead attitude and tendency to clutter.

Carole paused at the door. "Izzy?"

Izzy looked longingly at the desk. "No problem. I'll be right out." She grabbed the stack of telephone messages from on top of the computer, intending to return the calls between checking out books.

Straddling the stool behind the counter, Izzy keyed in the author, Bombeck, and allowed her eyes to roam over the mahogany bookshelves and vaulted ceiling. Mayhill Library had opened its doors in 1911, and until last year, little had changed. Izzy was fascinated by the still-talked-about exploits of the first librarian, Rosemary Mayhill, who had started the library with just two hundred books. For forty-one years Rosemary—now honored via a huge painting that hung behind the check-in desk—had added books to the shelves from her own funds and invited migrant workers to come in on Monday evenings to learn to read. Catherine Wilfong had taken over in 1952. Carole Martin had been in charge for the last six years. When Izzy had been hired, temporarily, her task was to bring the library into the twenty-first century. A happy glow tinted Izzy's cheeks. She hadn't changed the library's personality, she'd just made it more user-friendly. It had taken months of heated debate to convince Carole's husband to appropriate funds for updating the library. Only after Izzy convinced Carole of the need to modernize had part-time Mayor Jake Martin agreed to consider allotting tax dollars to technology.

Jake didn't like change. He wanted the library and his wife to stay exactly the same. After all, he was demonstrating his liberalism by letting Carole work. Before Catherine retired, he'd allowed Carole to make the long drive to Lincoln to take the necessary classes to qualify for a degree in library science.

Izzy always winced when Carole told the story and used the word *allowed*. If Jake had been Izzy's husband, he'd have walked around with a frying-pan necklace for most of his days.

A blue-haired woman pushed two romances and a home decorating book across the counter. "Hello, Izzy."

Izzy took the books. "Hello, Mrs. Hepfield. How are you today?"

"Call me Agatha and not so good, but I don't want to talk about it." The woman rolled her eyes then forced a smile before saying, "I'm so pleased that you've painted the children's area. Those crayons with the names of books instead of the names of colors are just a marvelous idea."

"Thank you, Agatha." Izzy felt a tinge of regret. She'd miss this place when she went home.

"Yes, I like the changes." Agatha reached over and laid her hand over Izzy's. "Rosemary would be proud of you."

"You knew Rosemary?" Izzy exclaimed, but Agatha was already walking away—her aged ears beyond hearing.

Mondays were typically slow. Izzy completed her phone calls and began pricing some of the books she intended to add to the back room where used paperbacks were sold. Carole sorted books. The sounds of Whip Thompson snoring over a newspaper added to the atmosphere.

The swish of the front door opening didn't inspire Izzy to

look up. That door would open a hundred more times this day without her noticing.

"Excuse me." A deep voice said.

Izzy looked up. The man, carrying a stack of at least fifteen books, towered over Carole. His rugged features spoke of hard work and hours in the sun. The arms that held the books balanced the load easily. Izzy bit her lip. She'd been in Mayhill almost two years. No way could she have missed this man. He handed Carole two books, stretching out a tanned, bare arm—taut with muscles—that captured Izzy eyes.

Carole grinned up at him. "Parker Strickland," she scolded. "I'll bet you haven't been in a library since high school."

"Only once or twice," he acknowledged, balancing the stack of books.

Carole took a few off the top and loaded them into the cart, managing to fumble a few onto the carpet.

He dumped the rest of them in a cluttered pile and bent down to retrieve the dropped books. He glanced around the library as if trying to decide if he wanted to stay. His brown eyes stopped their surveillance when they came in contact with Izzy's. Interest flashed, but quickly disappeared, momentarily replaced by a guarded look that tugged at Izzy's heart.

"This is Isobelle de la Rosa," Carole introduced, drawing Izzy close. "She's Clara Bryant's daughter."

Parker Strickland nodded, a handful of reddish-brown hair finding its way to his brow before he brushed it back. "Pleased to meet you."

Carole began checking the books. "Parker, these are way overdue!"

A frown marred his handsome features. "How much?"

"Let's see. Some were due. . .Parker! These are more than two years overdue!"

His frown deepened. "How much?"

"The ones that are years overdue we charge the price of the book," Izzy said, stepping closer. "The others are just a nickel a day."

"How much?" Parker repeated, pulling out his checkbook.

Carole ignored the computer and figured the total on the library's ancient calculator. "It's one hundred and fifty-two dollars."

He wrote the check without flinching, although Izzy thought she saw a moment of anger highlight his expression. This man hid his emotions well. He handed the payment to Carole and nodded good-bye.

The women watched him walk away. "His wife died a few years ago," Carole confided in a practiced whisper. "He just moved back to town."

Izzy stared after the man. The sadness that leapt from his eyes haunted her. This man didn't know the happiness the Lord could bring. He leaned against the wall, skimming one of the upcoming events announcements promoting the Mayhill Centennial. Folding it, he put it in his pocket before walking out the door.

"He's a looker." Carole hadn't missed Izzy's interest. "I've known his family for years." She moved closer to Izzy, her expression full of eagerness. There was nothing Carole enjoyed more than sharing the joys and sorrows of the Mayhill townsfolk. "Oops." Carole bent. "Missed one." She held up another book that had tumbled out of her grasp as Parker handed them to her. "Wait, this isn't one of ours." Carole frowned as she turned a blue book from front to back in her hands. "Here." She thrust the book toward Izzy.

From one glance, Izzy knew the book didn't belong in the library. It was a journal. She kept one herself. Only instead of a plain, blue cover, hers depicted a Victorian woman, sitting in a garden, head bent while writing.

"Is this Mr. Strickland's?" Izzy asked.

"I think so, but I didn't look."

Izzy opened the journal, intending to see if the front page identified the owner. Instead of a name, the first paragraph jumped out at her, a brittle scrawl that took up too much space, the tips of the letters sharp with anger.

I made it through another day. Another day. I think I'll make it through tomorrow. The next day—I'm not too sure about. I have the gun. I can use the gun. If I can't make it through the week.

The journal dropped from her hands as if it had suddenly turned hot. Izzy closed her eyes, feeling the color drain from her face. For a moment, she thought she heard the sound of her father's laughter.

Carole stared at the journal, concerned. "Well, is it Parker's?"

"I don't know. There's no name." Izzy picked up the book, deliberating about whether to share what she'd read.

"Never thought he looked like the type to keep a journal." Carole moved closer, eyeing the book with interest.

"Why not?" Izzy held the journal firmly.

"I've known him all my life. He's older than my Tom. Still, they played baseball, basketball, football. Never seen either of them crack a book. Of course, Parker went off to college. Maybe he developed the habit there."

The book felt brittle in Izzy's hands. Suddenly, she didn't want to claim possession of such private thoughts. "I'll see if I can catch up with Mr. Strickland."

Carole nodded, moving out of the way.

Izzy sprinted across the new mauve carpeting, pushed the library door open, and dashed across the grassy landscape of Mayhill Park. Parker Strickland was climbing into a pickup. Trucks seemed to be the vehicle of choice for Mayhill, Nebraska, men. Her small car always appeared dwarfed in the parking spaces. The men who asked her out always seemed surprised when she turned them down, as if the size of their vehicles should impress her. Instead, as she drove through the streets, she felt very much like the mechanical rabbit the greyhounds chased. A small morsel to be won.

"Mr. Strickland! Mr. Strickland!" she called.

Parker had one foot on the floorboard as he began to ease into his truck. He glanced back when he heard her.

"Mr. Strickland!" she called again.

"Yes."

"Is this yours?" She held up the journal.

Parker slowly took it, cracking it open. His eyes skimmed the page, and he frowned. "Oh, yeah, thanks." He tossed the journal on the passenger side. It skidded off the seat and landed on the floor. He climbed the rest of the way in.

Only after he started the engine and began to back out of his space did Izzy react. "Mr. Stickland," she said loudly, "are you okay?"

"Just dandy, ma'am." He shot her a puzzled glance as he drove away.

Izzy shook her head, thinking of what she had read in the journal. Someone should tell his family. She did bowl with his mother and father, but that wasn't enough to make her feel as if she knew them well. How could she confront mere acquaintances and confess that she'd gotten the information about their son from reading a page from his journal? Journals were supposed to be private. Parker Strickland had made it this long without her interference. Surely, he'd make it through the rest of the day while she considered what she might do. She headed back to the library, stopping under the big pin oak tree.

"Hi, Miss Izzy." Billy McKenna grinned toothlessly at her. Delta, his mother, read a book at a nearby park bench while Billy played in the falling leaves of September. School had started last week, making the park a daytime shrine to peace and quiet—except for the occasional toddler who rambled along the play area followed by a mother.

Izzy smiled at Delta and tousled Billy's hair, enjoying the childish texture of his deep brown curls. The sun shone down and highlighted hints of red in Billy's silken strands.

"You okay?" Delta put her book down and pushed a strand of blond hair from her eyes.

"Just thinking."

Delta took a deep breath and looked around with appreciation. "This is my favorite time of the year."

Izzy nodded and watched as a yellow and red leaf swirled

gracefully to the ground. How different this land was from Arizona. It was just six years ago, during a 122-degree summer heat spell, that she had sat across from her mother at the kitchen table trying to convince Mom to do something. . .to live again. Izzy had been twenty and going to Arizona State University. Mom had been spending too much time alone. Izzy had forced her mother to leave Phoenix to go on that cruise.

"Mom, you need to explore," a much younger Izzy had argued. "Get away from the doing the same old thing day in and day out."

"I'm fine," Clara de la Rosa had protested, staring with dismay at the airplane ticket that would transport her to California. "You want me to go alone?"

"This is a cruise for people your age." Izzy had encouraged, adding, "You'll have a blast!"

"I don't want to be with strangers," Clara had protested. Three weeks later, Izzy had kissed her protesting mother good-bye at Arizona's Sky Harbor Airport. Clara had grumbled, handing the stewardess her boarding pass and declining to check in her old, avocado suitcase. She clutched her luggage in an unwilling fist and refused to wave to Izzy.

The cruise had worked too well. First, her mother had phoned from Mexico, bubbling incoherent praises about a man named Harve. Next, two days after Clara should have been home, the sounds of celebration came over the phone, and suddenly Izzy had a stepfather. Clara moved out of the hot, desert mobile home in Apache Junction, a retirement community east of Phoenix, and traveled to the grasslands of the Midwest with her new husband.

Despite her reservations, Izzy liked Nebraska. Every summer since her mother's marriage, she'd left the heat of Phoenix and flown to Mayhill. But she'd never dreamed that one day she'd leave the malls and sunshine of Phoenix to reside in a town of a mere twenty thousand hardy souls who barely noticed the deep chill of winter that blanketed their town almost six months of the year. Two years ago, when

Clara had suffered a heart attack, Izzy had packed up and moved without regret. Nothing could replace family, and Mom was all she had left.

That was all in the past. Mom had been walking every day, and now she and Harve were in Florida attending his oldest daughter's wedding. Then, they were off to Kentucky to spend time with his other daughter and her family.

Izzy was free to go back home. But she couldn't, not until Carole had her baby. When Izzy had first arrived in Mayhill, all she had done was take care of her mother. After six months, things had calmed down, and Izzy had applied at the city hall. She'd been thinking of taking a clerical job for a while. But Mayor Martin had happened upon her resume, and instead of a job she could easily walk away from, she'd started at the library.

"It's just temporary," Mayor Martin had insisted. Reluctantly, Izzy tried to pretend that she hadn't locked herself into a situation that she'd have a hard time escaping. But escape it she would, as soon as Carole ended her maternity leave.

A gust of wind shook Izzy from her wonderings. The leaves rolled against her shoes. A vibrant variation of red, gold, green, and yellow marked the changing of the season.

"Billy, stop that!" Delta's voice came loudly. Billy plopped to the ground at the base of the big tree in the middle of the park, its lowest limb out of his reach.

"Aw, Mom," he whined. "All the kids climb this tree. I want to."

"You're not old enough." Delta looked her son up and down. "Or tall enough."

"How's Billy liking kindergarten?" Izzy asked.

"He loves it. I took him out early today for a doctor's appointment. I didn't see any reason to take him back. Besides, there'll only be a few more days like this before snow."

"God truly made a beautiful day." Izzy nodded and looked at her watch. "I've got to get back to work. See you." Briskly, she headed toward the library.

Carole looked up, worried, when Izzy breezed through the double doors.

"Was it his?"

"Yes." Izzy leaned against a shelf. "Is he always that sad?"

"I thought he was doing better. Today must have been a bad shift. He's a fireman."

Izzy thought about those broad shoulders. A fireman? That made sense. She'd feel perfectly safe if he scooped her up and carried her down a ladder. Unbidden, the image of the corded muscles of his arms flashed though her mind, and Izzy sat down on the stool with a thud. *Where did that thought come from?*

Carole looked around the silent library, then said suddenly. "Parker met his wife in college. Julia died coming back from Lincoln during a snowstorm. Parker blames himself. He seems to think that if he had been with her the accident wouldn't have happened."

Captivated, Izzy stopped rearranging. "Would it have?"

"Julia was from southern California. She didn't know how to drive in the snow. From what Parker's mother told me, he'd asked Julia to stay home that day, but she'd wanted to go shopping. Imagine that! Risking a blizzard to buy a new dress." Carole opened her mouth, as if she had something more to say, but thought better of it. "Let's just say she wasn't used to taking the weather into consideration."

Izzy nodded. Parker Strickland obviously wasn't over his wife's death, not if he wrote such dismal entries in his journal.

❧

Parker hated days off. He would just as soon work and keep his mind occupied. Mayhill didn't have many fires, but he doubled as a paramedic, and that kept him busy. Two months ago he'd participated in the community effort to save the livestock of the area's farmers. He, Jeff Henly, and Ty Horner had driven to farm after farm and turned the hose on panting animals, hoping to keep them from dying of heat. When winter rolled around, there'd be other emergencies such as downed power lines and distant residents unable to drive to the hospital.

He flicked the turn signal on, heading for Summers Cafe. He'd grab a late lunch and then go to his parents' house. As he turned the corner, the blue book that librarian had returned to him slid toward his boot.

Parker shook his head, bending to retrieve the journal. He wished the librarian had thrown it away.

He thought he caught a whiff of that librarian. . .what was her name? Isobelle de la Rosa? Her perfume lingered around the book. She didn't look anything like her mother. Parker remembered when Harve had brought Clara home. The community had been in an uproar for months. They hadn't quite recovered from the knowledge that a retired, widowed farmer would even want to take a cruise before Harve returned with a big-city bride. Parker recalled seeing Izzy a few times when she'd been in Mayhill visiting her mother. He'd been happily married to Julia then. He wondered how he'd missed seeing her around town since he'd moved back, then reconsidered. He didn't frequent any of the places singles hung out.

Was she single?

It bothered him that the urge to find out her marital status crossed his mind.

Isobelle had been cute. She'd tripped across the park's grass in high heels with beige pants hugging an athletic build. She looked healthy enough, but health wasn't enough to battle cold Nebraskan winters. He recalled how the wind had caught the fringed vest she'd worn, blowing it back so that her white shirt was exposed to contrast with her tan neck. She lived up to her name, de la Rosa. She smelled like a rose. Her long, black hair, high cheekbones, and olive complexion spoke of distant ancestors, rich in Hispanic blood and mystique.

Parker looked out the side window and slammed on his brakes. He'd been thinking about the librarian and driven right past the cafe. He didn't care if she were single or not!

He turned the truck around and finally pulled into one of the cafe's parking places. The journal fell back to the floor.

Parker pushed it under the seat. He would deal with it later. Izzy was nothing like Julia, that was for sure. Parker sat in the truck, staring at the cafe. He'd lost his appetite. What was it that woman had called after him? "Mr. Strickland, are you okay?" Hah, she had called him mister. She must think he was fifty years old.

"Just dandy," he'd answered.

He had lied.

&

"Has Parker Strickland gone to counseling?" Izzy fed Mr. Whiskers, the library's rabbit. It had been hours since the fireman had left, yet she couldn't get him off her mind.

Carole raised an eyebrow. "What for?"

"The grief from dealing with the loss of his wife."

"I don't know. He's been away for so long. He moved to Lincoln, went to school, and now he's back. Say," Carole filed the audio cassettes in the bin. "You're sure asking a lot of questions. Has he gone and sparked your interest?"

Izzy tried to smile. She'd overdone the questions. She should have known better. What else was Carole to think with Izzy prying into the fireman's history?

"No, no, please don't get any matchmaking ideas. I was just curious, that's all. I thought I'd met just about everyone in this town."

"He's Kenny Latkam's cousin."

Izzy took a step back.

"I know," Carole laughed. "Those two boys are as opposite as can be. Kenny's an only child, and then there's just Parker and his sister. Their parents doted on them. Parker and Rhea turned out okay. Oh, sure, Parker sowed his wild oats. But Kenny, whew, I wouldn't let my daughter within ten feet of him! He finally stopped bothering you, didn't he?"

"After I filed a complaint with the sheriff."

"Kenny wouldn't hurt a fly. He's just spoiled rotten. It's probably a good thing he's leaving town. He and his cousin Chris used to get in more trouble. . . ."

Izzy nodded, not really listening, but glad that Carole's thoughts had shifted from Parker Strickland to his cousin and away from Izzy's interest in the fireman.

When school let out, the patronage doubled. Gum-smacking students prowled the aisles, looking for term-paper material. Already the *Phantom of the Opera* video was in demand. A quick-fingered senior boy with hair longer than Izzy's had snagged it at five minutes after three, and now twelve names graced the reserved list. It looked as if Mayhill seniors intended to avoid reading the book. A tall football player frowned brutally at the card catalogue, roughly shoving in a drawer and turning to glare at Izzy as if she'd purposely hidden the card for whatever book it was he wanted. Izzy hoped he'd be kinder to the computers after they were installed.

At seven o'clock Izzy played the recording bidding the final patrons farewell and put the monies collected for fines into the safe. When everyone was gone, she checked on the rabbit, set the alarm, and followed Carole out the back door.

Izzy didn't go straight home on Mondays. In order to get to know the town and its people, she had followed her mother's example and made an effort to get involved with the community. Bowling seemed an easy way to make friends, so she'd let her landlord, Whip Thompson, talk her into joining his league. Now she had more friends over sixty-five than she knew what to do with. Her collection of crocheted washcloths was extensive, and if her car ever decided to break down, a flock of undershirted men appeared like vultures to surround the dead machine and debate. The more she got to know her parents' friends the more she liked them, although she did long for friends her own age. She missed Connie Decker, her best friend back in Phoenix. Connie didn't bowl, she was into twelve-step programs, usually having to do with diets. Connie didn't crochet washcloths, she collected dolls. Connie had never read a book from the comfort of a park bench or stopped to watch red and yellow leaves fall to the ground. She was too busy supervising the day-care center at church.

Izzy hated being torn between two places.

Tonight, watching her team members laugh and talk about their day, Izzy felt out of sorts. She kept an eye on Francine and Blake Strickland, looking for some indication that they were worried about their son. Nothing. The two wore matching green sweaters and looked as if they could pose for a seniors' fitness magazine. They didn't notice her stares.

Izzy missed picking up the ten pin by inches. Whip sent his ball down the alley for a strike. Her game was off, but that made sense. For the first time in over a year, her mind was on a member of the male sex. With a half-smile, she thought back to the guys she'd dated since moving to Mayhill. Most of them very nice, but nobody with enough charisma to keep her from concentrating on striving for that 300 bowling score. Until Parker Strickland. And it wasn't his charisma she was worried about.

"Where's your mind tonight, girl?" grumped Whip after Izzy missed an easy spare.

"You feeling all right?" asked Agatha, wiping her bowling ball off with a crocheted towel. It was embarrassing. Tonight both Agatha and Whip had bowled better than she, and Agatha's ball weighed barely six pounds.

"Just a long day," Izzy replied.

When the final game ended, Izzy removed her bowling shoes, struggling with the nagging feeling that she needed to do something. She, alone, knew that Parker Strickland was suicidal, and instead of seeking the man out and talking to him, she'd gone bowling. She stopped at the public telephone just inside the bowling alley's entryway and looked up Parker's address and phone number. She wrote it down on the receipt part of her checkbook. His house was miles out of town.

Izzy pulled out of the parking lot and drove to the corner. Checking her watch, she bit her lip. It was just after ten. She just needed to make sure he was okay. Otherwise, she wouldn't get any sleep. She turned away from her own home and headed toward Parker Strickland's address.

The road was void of streetlights. Izzy relied on the moon and her headlights glancing off fields and trees. In a way, driving through the rural roads at night seemed an adventure. She squinted, trying to see, but the darkness settled around Parker's place, making everything a silhouette. All she could tell was that it was a large farm. As she came closer, she noted that lights burned in almost every window. Izzy checked her watch, not surprised that the man was awake. She had once dated a military fireman and knew they kept erratic hours. She drove past the house and turned into a side driveway, backed up, and turned the car toward home. To her dismay, Parker Strickland came out of his house and stood on the porch with his hands on his hips. He'd seen her, and since she had driven past the McKennas' place, he knew whoever was on his road must be visiting him.

Wishing she was anywhere else, Izzy considered driving by. She could put her foot to the gas and zoom by. He might not notice who she was. With sinking heart, Izzy realized he'd know her car. Everybody knew her car. Maybe it was time to get rid of the Peugeot and get a truck. No, that would mean she was adapting to small-town America.

She inched closer to his house, and he stepped off his porch, sauntering to the road and her car. Izzy braked and leaned over to roll down the passenger side window.

Parker bent, crossing his arms over the door. "You lost, Ms. de la Rose?"

"It's Miss de la Rosa and, no, I'm not lost." The minute the words left her mouth, Izzy wanted them back. He'd just given her the perfect reason for being on a seldom-used back road. She'd blown it. "I'm not lost," she repeated. "I–I–I just came out here to tell you that you owe another two dollars worth of fines on those library books."

two

Dark branches waved with the wind behind Parker. His face didn't change expression as he reached in his back pocket and withdrew his wallet to extract two dollars. "You drove all the way out here to collect a library fine?"

"Carole said you hardly ever use our facilities. I wanted to make sure you were aware of our policy."

Parker laid the money on the passenger seat. "A simple overdue notice would have sufficed." He stepped back, shoved his hands in his back pockets, and studied her car.

"What's wrong?" she said.

"This car's going to be useless in the winter."

"Don't worry about me. I don't go far." The pane of glass slid into position. Izzy pushed on the gas and drove away, watching Parker in the rearview mirror. He stood in his front yard, an unyielding, diminishing figure.

"I can't believe what I just did," Izzy mourned aloud, embarrassment making her hands shake. Why had she driven out to his house? What had possessed her? Even worse, the bad feeling in her gut did not go away. Her foot hovered over the brake, then settled on it. "Okay, Lord, I'm pretty sure what You'd do. It's not as if he can embarrass me any further tonight." She turned the car around. "And just maybe I can help him."

All his lights were still on. Izzy pulled into the driveway. She sat a moment, contemplating, then grabbed the two dollars from the passenger seat and stepped out of the car.

As if he'd been waiting for her, Parker came out the screen door and stood at the edge of the porch. His hands were jabbed tightly in his pockets. He didn't look as if the word *welcome* was in his vocabulary.

20

She made it all the way to the bottom step before he spoke. "Do I owe more money or are you lost?"

Izzy took a breath. "Neither." She held out the two dollars. "I don't make it a habit to lie. You made me nervous, and I said the first thing that came to my mind. You didn't owe the library two dollars. Please, take it back."

He took his hands out of his pocket and crossed them over his chest. He reminded her of her father. The stance he'd taken whenever she was trying to tell him why she'd missed curfew; why she'd gotten a C on her report card; why she thought it was okay to wear makeup.

"Look," Izzy went on quickly, waving the money as if it were a white flag. "I'm really embarrassed. I came out here to see if you were okay."

"Okay? Why wouldn't I be okay?"

"Well, you know, you acted a little funny today at the library. Kind of sad."

"Oh, and you follow sad people home from the library?"

"I didn't follow you home!" Izzy stepped back.

"No?"

"I went bowling, and then I looked your address up in the phone book."

"All because you were worried about me?"

Izzy smiled hopefully and nodded. Surely, he would remember that he had turned in the journal and what was written on the first page. "Yes, all because I was worried about you. Do you need any help?"

"What kind of help are you offering?" He stepped to the edge of the porch.

Too close in Izzy's opinion. She took a breath. Every fiber of her being told her she was safe, but still she felt vulnerable standing in Mr. Strickland's front yard. "Maybe I could arrange for one of the deacons at my church to come have a Bible study with you. You'd be surprised at how—"

"No, that won't be necessary," Parker said slowly. "I'm fine. Nothing to worry about. I don't need your help."

She had no choice. The man obviously was annoyed with her. Sticking around would only annoy him more. Izzy forced the two dollars in his hand, ignoring the shiver that ignited when his warm fingers closed over hers. She yanked her hand away and hurried back to her car. As she pulled back out onto the dirt road, she didn't allow herself to look back. She was too afraid she'd see the man laughing.

Lord, I could have handled that better. One more chapter in the story of Isobelle de la Rosa's life. Forever acting on impulse and repenting at leisure. Paul wrote to the Ephesians, "Therefore do not be foolish, but understand what the Lord's will is." Izzy took a deep breath. A carefully constructed plan would have worked better with Parker, instead of a late-night spontaneous encounter. Well, she'd put him on the church's prayer list and see what happened.

She calmed down as she drove through the silent night and entered the city limit. In Phoenix, even this late, the roads would be busy. She waited at the stoplight in the center of town, noticing a few cars still in the Summers Cafe parking lot. The place doubled as a club at night, but she'd never been there. The light turned green, and she drove the last block to her apartment. Whip owned a white clapboard two-story Victorian. Izzy had almost refused to rent from him once she found that they had to share a kitchen, but she'd fallen in love with the home when he showed her around.

She pulled into the driveway and sat in the car a moment. The porch light burned, bidding her enter. None of the downstairs lamps were on, except for the kitchen's. It looked as if she'd manage to catch Whip asleep. He was a great landlord. An angel in disguise. Within a month of her moving in, he'd convinced her to participate in a weekly Bible study, taught her how to make banana bread, and coached her in the intricacies of playing checkers.

Izzy often came home to find a casserole warming in the oven or a plate of meat loaf with her name written on a paper napkin in the refrigerator. Sharing a kitchen wasn't half bad.

Whip assured her that if she wanted privacy all she had to do was notify him in advance, and he'd spend the evening at his son's house. Izzy couldn't imagine telling the man to leave his own home, since he'd been nothing but polite to the few visitors she'd had. When her best friend Connie had come for a visit, he'd taken her all around while Izzy worked. Connie had gone back to Arizona spouting wheat prices and wearing a John Deere hat.

Izzy let herself in through the back door that opened into the kitchen. A piece of peach pie waited on the table. She poured a glass of milk and sat down with fork in hand. If Whip kept up the culinary treats, she'd soon be forced to buy a new wardrobe. A size bigger! The sugary goodness had a calming effect, helping her to pretend that tonight hadn't been a complete fiasco. She knew Parker Strickland was still alive. Alive and *alone* in a distant farmhouse.

She finished the peach pie and climbed the stairs to her apartment. Her living room light glowed. Izzy knew she'd left it off and felt fairly certain that Whip had stolen up here to make sure she didn't enter a dark room. She shrugged out of her sweater, not sure if she liked her landlord acting like a parent. After a year of living with her mother and Harve, she had moved to Whip's upstairs apartment to regain independence and sanity. Radar meowed from the flowered couch, blinking away the effects of sleep and jumping down to wind his way around her feet.

"Did Whip feed you?" Izzy asked as she turned on the television.

The big black and white cat got up on his hind legs, patting Izzy's knees, informing her that he wanted to be carried. She picked him up and walked into the bathroom, checking his food bowl, not surprised to find fresh water and an open can of cat food. Lately, Whip had started cooking liver for Radar. It was only a matter of time before the feline began to share residency with the man downstairs.

She changed into her pajamas. Picking up her Bible, she

settled down on the couch. She had been reading the Old Testament, but for some reason, tonight Izzy felt more inclined to turn to the writings of Paul.

Paul was her favorite apostle, along with Peter. They made mistakes, yet knew truth when it stared them in the face. Idly, Izzy stroked Radar's soft fur as she read about the cost of being a disciple. She wondered what Paul would say to Parker? What advice would the apostle give? One thing for sure, Izzy couldn't forget the lost look in Parker's eyes. Nor could she forget the warmth of his touch on her fingers. Somehow, Izzy knew, she had to help him.

He must have adored his wife.

Izzy knew what it felt like to love and lose. She knew what it was like to have the floor ripped from under her. Without her family and the Lord, she'd have been lost. Her weekly Bible study with Whip had brought her even closer to knowing peace. Parker had family, but he didn't seem to have the Lord.

Izzy fell asleep in the living room with her Bible open, the light on, and the television blaring.

❧

Parker stayed outdoors for a long time, sitting on the front porch. After Julia died, friends had taken to visiting at odd hours. He'd never invited anyone but family into the house. After realizing a visit to Parker's meant standing in the front yard, the visits had tapered off.

He'd been watching television when he'd seen the car lights coming up his road. He'd recognized her Peugeot. With mixed emotions he'd gotten off the couch and walked outside to wait. For a moment he'd thought she wouldn't stop. As he'd walked to her car, he'd told himself to be polite, neighborly, invite her to sit on the porch. But the minute his mouth opened, the habit of misery had made itself known, and he'd been indifferent to her, making sure no one got close to him again.

He'd known from the start that she had not driven all that way to tell him he owed the library a two-dollar fine, but this business about his being sad didn't reason out either. He wasn't sure what she was after.

What a crazy day. What really bothered him was that she'd been on his mind since he'd left the library. Her scent had lingered in his memory all day. It had stayed with him during lunch and when he went over to his parents' house. It was great to be back in Mayhill and with family. All he needed was to keep busy and be with family, even if his family included his worthless cousin Kenny.

Kenny! Now there was a mess. Parker had spent a good part of the morning cleaning the one-room garage apartment Kenny rented from Agatha Hepfield. He'd packed the old clothes, thrown out all the newspapers, and gotten rid of the furniture. Kenny had done nothing but take what little he'd thought he'd need at boot camp. From what Parker understood, Kenny had spent the night in town with some woman instead of with his family. Kenny deserved boot camp in Parker's opinion. At least the town would get some peace. And maybe Kenny would grow up. The apartment had been a mess with half-eaten food cemented to plates under the bed. Dried milk had added permanent stains to glasses littering the dresser. Plates amassed with stubby cigarette butts tumbled old ashes onto Parker's fingers. Agatha had appeared at the door numerous times, shaking her head in sorrow and looking as if she might cry. Parker shooed her away and spent the entire morning clearing out that one small room, and the only reason he'd done it was because he didn't want his aunt Edna to see further proof of what a slob her son was. If Kenny hadn't already left, Parker would have hunted him down.

After finishing Kenny's apartment, Parker had dropped off the books at the library, grabbed lunch, and then stopped off at his parents. His parents' house had not been a place of joy. He'd hoped to drop off some of Kenny's belongings without having to face Edna, but Aunt Edna had been sitting in the living room, weeping over the indignities her son might suffer in the military.

"Kenny should have gone to college," she had sniffed into her tissue.

"Now," Parker's mother patted her sister on the shoulder, "lots of boys choose the service as a way to see the world." Francine Strickland had looked up, her gaze falling on Parker, and said, "Parker thought about it for a while. His dad and I told him it was up to him. He happened to choose college."

Aunt Edna glared at Parker, her frown suggesting that if he'd chosen the service, Kenny would not have followed in his footsteps. "He applied for a position with the city. I don't know why he wasn't hired."

"I have some of his stuff in the back of my truck. You want me to load it in your car?" Parker wasn't about to inform Aunt Edna that Kenny's police record kept him from being considered for the fire department's opening. Too many of the powers that be knew Kenny's disposition and, although they felt bad for Edna, they believed the good of the community would be threatened if Kenny were to don a fireman's uniform. Not that Kenny could have passed the oral interview, anyway. It was just dumb luck that had Parker taking the position Edna wanted for her son.

"It's unlocked." Edna waved her sodden handkerchief.

Parker carried three boxes over to Edna's car.

"Parker, you staying for supper?" Mom asked.

Parker rubbed his stomach, mumbled about eating at Summers, and casting a wary eye at Aunt Edna, left.

A farmhouse full of memories awaited him at home. Memories stamped with the exquisite taste of his wife. He remembered her excitement. She'd so loved the rolling countryside that she'd sat right down at the kitchen table after they'd gotten married and wrote down a list of everything she wanted for the farm. Half the things they didn't need, like a tractor. Other things, like a horse, would surprise her when it came time to actually caring for the animal. Parker had put her off with the excuse of time.

"We'll get these things one at a time," he'd assured her, and she'd wrapped her arms around his neck in happiness. Now as he lived in the farmhouse alone, he wished he'd given her everything.

No wonder Isobelle de la Rosa's visit had him pondering. The library definitely rated as the high point of the day. Parker stood up. Leaving his musings on the front porch, he entered the silent house. Blinking his eyes against the glare of the television, he realized he wasn't a bit sleepy.

Two hours later, Parker carried the last box of Julia's knick-knacks out to the shed. He'd gone through every room, packed her personal belongings and taken down all her pictures, save the three on the living room wall. Undoubtedly, he'd done enough packing today. Maybe it was time to let go a little. He undressed in the living room. He hadn't slept in the bedroom since Julia had. . .left. Even when he'd moved to Lincoln to finish his schooling and attempt to leave Julia's memories behind, he'd found himself not liking to sleep in the bedroom. Couches were much more comfortable. There, he never turned in the middle of the night to reach out only to discover an empty half of the bed.

He slept lightly, partly from habit, partly from training. The rooster over at McKennas' place woke him. Parker's mouth felt dry. Wearily, he rolled off the couch and went to the kitchen for something to drink. Sitting at the table meant for two, he downed a glass of milk. His dreams had awakened him too often during the night. Oddly, Isobelle had been in them, not his wife. Her late-night visit had stayed on his mind longer than he wanted. There was no reason for an absolute stranger to affect him. Why had she *really* driven out to the farm? He quickly washed his glass before heading to the bedroom to dress. Looking in the mirror he saw a man who didn't need anybody. A man who could only bear to lose a love— once.

Parker pulled a dark blue T-shirt over his head. He'd avoid that woman like the plague, even if her perfume made him want to sing.

Izzy loved being first to the library in the morning. She liked turning the lights on and finding the books standing up straight in military rows, acting as if they'd protected the building during the midnight hours. She liked the waiting smell of a room that was built for the sole purpose of having people stroll over its carpeting as they contemplated their next written-word adventure.

"Good morning, Rosemary." She greeted the painting of the first librarian. "What did you read overnight?" Izzy leaned forward, pretending to listen. "What? You read the Bible?" Looking around, Izzy confided, "Me, too."

Izzy went around the building, checking to make sure everything was in its place. She started the coffeemaker and went into the office to attempt clearing off Carole's desk. She'd be alone with only a student worker once Carole went on leave; neither volunteers nor insurance were part of the Mayhill Library budget. She had to get everything in order.

The rattling of a key announced Carole's entrance. Izzy smiled, listening as Carole silently put away her purse and sneaked to the back room to pour a much-needed cup of coffee.

"One, two, three," Izzy counted, imagining Carole taking a drink at every number, gradually waking up.

Finally, Carole passed by the office door on her way to the overnight drop box to collect the books that had been returned after hours. "Morning, boss." Carole kidded. Seeing Izzy seated at the desk never bothered the head librarian.

Izzy waved as the phone rang. The morning started with a conversation with Jake Martin, transitioned into updating files and ended with a phone call from one of the librarians from the University at Lincoln. They were putting together a list of Nebraska authors. Izzy was double-checking the spelling of the G authors when Carole stuck her head in and smiled. "You ready for lunch?"

Four hours had passed!

"Or do you want me to go first?" Carole rubbed her stomach.

"Are you hungry?"

"Well, Jake said that if I managed to get away at noon, he'd meet me."

Izzy glanced at her watch. "You go ahead. I'll go when you return."

There were two patrons in the library, and a sleeping Whip was one. Delta McKenna was the other. As soon as Delta selected and checked out her choice, Izzy was on her toes, ushering her friend out the door. Checking to make sure Whip still slept, she headed for the microfiche files and looked up the last five years of the *Mayhill Daily*. She sat before the terminal and chewed her bottom lip. Should she look up Parker's past in the local newspaper? Would finding out more about him help her figure out why he had written such dismal words in his journal?

Izzy sneaked another glance at Whip. The library was part of his morning ritual. He slumped in the chair, chin resting on his shirt as his chest rose and fell with reassuring snores. Izzy inserted the fiche and began. Julia Strickland glowed from the page of marriage announcements. She and Parker had married during their junior year, before he'd even graduated from the University of Nebraska in Lincoln. The small-town paper burst with news about the couple's early days. Izzy followed the newlyweds through the purchase of the farm, and Julia's first automobile wreck—which had taken place during the winter and on to. . .

"What are you doing?" Carole interrupted, breathing over Izzy's shoulder. "Hmmm, checking up on Parker?"

"I was just curious," Izzy defended herself, jumping up and knocking her pencil to the floor.

"If I were single, I'd be more than curious."

Izzy tried to act nonchalant as she switched off the scanner. "He was cute. I just thought I'd check him out."

Carole dropped onto the chair at the next computer and lifted her blond hair high. "What do you want to know?"

"How depressed has he been since his wife passed away?"

"Oh, Izzy. What a question! He took it hard, of course. Who wouldn't? He's done okay. I think it was smart of him to get away for a couple of years. His ma wasn't too happy that he didn't come home more often, Lincoln only being a few hours away, but now she's proud of him. He trained to receive his emergency care license while there. Rhea McCoy's his sister, and he's related to the Walker brood over in Waco, Nebraska. It's about seventy miles east of here. You've heard of Chris? The one who ran around with Kenny and caused all that trouble."

"I don't think I've met Chris Walker." Izzy bent and picked up her pencil. "Rhea's never mentioned that she had a brother."

"She has. You just don't remember. I guess you were too busy thinking about escaping back to Phoenix."

Whip snorted, stood up stiff-leggedly, and walked out the front door with a look of bemusement on his face.

Carole watched his progress with a giggle and went to get the spare newspaper. "You'd better go grab some lunch."

Izzy grabbed her purse, irritated that Whip might have been awake during their conversation about Parker's past. She walked out of the library as Carole reached for the phone. What Izzy needed was chocolate. What she didn't need was for the whole town to know that she was checking up on Parker.

After sliding into a booth at Summers, Izzy studied the menu she already knew by heart. The noise of camaraderie echoed around her. Most of the time she packed a lunch and ate in the park, liking the company of birds and squirrels, but last night she'd been restless. She'd slept right through the alarm this morning, waking only after Whip had banged on the downstairs ceiling with a broom. Scrambling into her clothes, she hadn't even had the time to thank him for waking her, let alone prepare a lunch.

She watched the people, nodding at the ones who nodded to her. Did any of them know to worry about Parker? She ate quickly, paid the bill, and went out blinking into the sunlight.

Glancing at her watch, she realized that she had over twenty minutes before she needed to return to work. She started to step across the street to the park, thinking that she had plenty of work to do, but instead, as if guided by some unseen force, she headed for her car.

The fire station was three blocks away from the library. Izzy had driven by it numerous times without ever giving it a once over. She hunkered down, hoping to cruise by without attracting attention to herself. Ty Horner polished the already gleaming machine, while Jeff Henly seemed to be rolling the hose into some sort of doughnut shape. Both were testimonies to bodybuilding. They preened as water dripped down their muscles and soaked dark blue T-shirts. Izzy knew them. They made weekly trips to the library. It seemed that education and being a fireman went hand in hand. If they were the last ones in the library, they saw her safely to her car. They were both married, and at the moment their wives looked very much like Carole from the side view.

Parker sat alone on a bench in front of the brick building with the etched words *Mayhill Fire Station Number One*. It looked as if he was sewing the button onto some huge sort of jacket. His legs were stretched out before him, crossed at the ankles. He looked so alone. The comparison between the two laughing, wet firemen and Parker hit Izzy in the gut with all the finesse of a line drive. The man needed her help. No one else seemed to be paying any attention to him.

≈

Parker watched the Peugeot drive by with only the top of a jet black head visible. He'd glanced over at Ty and Jeff to see them switch from easy male bantering to flexing in the blink of an eye. Parker almost laughed at Ty using the firehose as a freeweight, but kept his face perfectly solemn as the woman whom he needed to ignore drove by. Just what was she doing? Why wasn't she sitting up? She could cause a wreck driving like that.

"I don't think she drove by for us." Ty turned the hose in

Parker's direction, purposely sending a spray of water at his friend's feet. "Just say the word, Parker. Jane and I will be glad to invite Izzy over. Help fix you two up."

"Doris says you had a whopping library fine," Jeff added from on top of the engine. "That's an expensive way to score a date. I think you might have a fighting chance."

"Izzy? She calls herself Izzy?" Parker grumbled at his mates, intent on convincing them that he had no interest in the woman. He didn't want her to be called Izzy. Izzy made him think of a warm woman in his arms, head thrown back as she smiled. Her wild, raven hair tempting him into commitment. Isobelle sounded more refined. More like someone he could keep at a distance.

"Yeah, Izzy." Jeff winked an eye. "She moved here a few months after you left. Her ma's Clara Bryant. You know, Harve's new wife. Izzy's kinda hard to get a handle on. I haven't seen her even once after hours at Summers Place. Of course that might be because your cousin Kenny was hassling her. Smart girl. She ran. Dad says she's a pretty good bowler."

Parker hadn't visited the Summers nighttime bar scene since he'd returned. He didn't want to answer questions or nod at people trying to express their concern with kind words.

So Izzy didn't bother going out either. She probably found the nightlife in Mayhill a little less invigorating than in Phoenix. *Isobelle,* he told himself, *I must think of her as Isobelle.*

"You don't need to worry about me. I'm not after her." Parker stood.

"You done?" Jeff looked at the turnout jacket.

"I'm done." Parker went inside, staying close enough to the open door to listen.

Jeff and Ty watched him, grinning. Parker went into the office and tried to read their lips through the glass.

"It's about time," Jeff was saying.

Ty cleared his throat. "He'll never do anything about—"

"Unless we help," Jeff finished.

Parker looked out the window and wondered why the two men were shaking hands.

◆

"I need part of tomorrow afternoon off." Carole peeked in the office door, looking almost afraid to enter.

"Are you okay?" Izzy taped clip art to her authors' flier. She'd finally finished it two days ago.

"I have a doctor's appointment at one. I'll return when it's over. Just think of it as my lunch hour."

Izzy looked up from the memo she'd received proclaiming that funds were unavailable for the computers she'd requested for library patron use. Mayor Martin wrote that the library's spending this past year already exceeded the former ten years and that it was time to limit funding. Izzy took off her glasses and rubbed her eyes. "Do we have anything planned?"

Carole shifted uneasily. "The kindergarten class from Mayhill Elementary is coming on a field trip."

"When did we schedule that? I'll be the only one here!"

"It's not that hard," Carole protested.

"I know it's not that hard, but what if somebody wanders in and needs assistance? I can't very well leave a class of five-year-olds in the middle of a fairy tale, now can I?"

"You won't be alone, the teacher will be here. And besides, our patrons are very patient. They'll realize that you're busy. Everyone knows I'm going to the doctor. You worry too much." Carole carefully turned and headed back to the front desk where Mrs. Hepfield waited.

Izzy brought up a new screen on her computer and began typing a reply to Jake Martin, citing statistics about the necessary skills needed by high schoolers and how computers were a must for employment and educational opportunities. Currently, Izzy knew the high school was scurrying to keep up with the latest technology. Izzy wanted to offer after-school tutoring about computer use, but without computers there could be no class. Mayor Martin needed to make some decisions fast. Izzy only intended to stay in Mayhill four more months. After the New Year, she was heading back to sunshine and no shoveling.

⁂

Chief Robert Parrish strolled into the fire station, checked the big calendar on the wall, and turned to Parker. "Are you on call tomorrow?"

"Yes." Parker looked up from his crossword puzzle. He had Monday off, but during the rotation of the four city employees, the man off duty remained on call.

"Your sister spoke to me at church this morning. She wants someone to come talk to the kindergarten class about fire safety. They plan to bring the kids here in a few months, so they don't need the engine. Since it's your sister's class, I thought you might like the assignment."

"No problem. I'll teach them to Stop, Drop, and Roll." Parker liked going to the schools. He'd always wanted children of his own, but he made do with Rhea bringing her two over to the farmhouse to explore the outdoors. He'd even fixed up the spare room with some of their toys for when they stayed over.

"Rhea wants you at her classroom about twelve-thirty." Robert penciled Parker's name on the duty roster and went to change clothes.

Jeff came in the back room and gathered up his lunchbox and belongings. "Going to the school tomorrow?"

"Yeah."

"Better you than me." Jeff took off the black boots he'd been wearing to wash the engine and put on his high-tops. He watched as Parker took his notebook out of the top pocket of his shirt to record tomorrow's appointment. "I just wish I could come along and watch you squirm."

"Squirm?" Parker said, raising an eyebrow.

Jeff chuckled as he left the room.

three

"What do you mean Delta McKenna canceled? I'm supposed to give a talk about fire safety, not chauffeur kids to and from the library." Parker felt himself growing agitated at the thought of facing Isobelle de la Rosa.

"Listen." Rhea McCoy shook a ruler at him, not looking the least bit sorry that she was putting him in a fix. "Delta said the vet was supposed to be there before noon, but he didn't show. She can't just leave. I need another driver, so big bro, since you're already here, it's gonna be you."

Parker looked around the classroom. Children sat on the floor, building with blocks or coloring in books. Others stared up at him with wide-eyed admiration. He felt trapped. Last week, he'd vowed not to go near Izzy, now his sister was forcing him to walk right into the crazy librarian's domain.

"All right! Everyone find their partners." Rhea clapped her hands. Immediately children started putting away the toys and grabbing for fingers. "Hold hands!"

Parker felt a tug on his thumb and looked down at one of the little boys Rhea had assigned to him. Billy McKenna stared up at him through inch-thick glasses. The boy was sucking his thumb and bending his knees in a weird aerobic bounce. "I gotta go to the bathroom," he chirped around his thumb.

"Take him, quickly," Rhea urged.

Parker walked with Billy down the hall and let him go unattended into the boy's room. Billy lived, with his mother and grandparents, at the farm next to Parker and spent a lot of time shooting plastic arrows at the trees behind Parker's field. Delta McKenna often moseyed into Parker's yard on the pretense of fetching Billy.

"You want me to fix you some supper, Parker?" Delta

would ask, her eyes hopeful. Parker might have been tempted. He had known Delta all his life. But her name was too closely linked to his cousin Chris's. There were those in town who spoke of the amazing resemblance of Billy's hair to that of Parker's cousin.

Rhea popped her head around the corner and shooed three more little boys in his direction. "They're riding with you."

Billy came out of the bathroom, holding his pants together until Parker could force the rusty snap to connect. He swung Billy up in his arms and walked out of the school building trailed by the rest of his passengers. If Billy was Chris's son, Chris didn't know what he was missing. In Parker's opinion, Billy was a great kid who needed more of a male influence.

"Are you really a fireman?" two boys asked in unison as Parker loaded them into his extended cab.

Billy answered. "Yes, he's really a fireman, and he gets to wash the big, red truck all the time. And he never has to wash dishes."

The other boys looked impressed. Parker blinked, amused that Billy was spending time peeking in the kitchen door when he wasn't shooting the plastic arrows. Turning the key in the ignition, Parker heard Billy add, "And he gets to slide down the pole."

Parker glanced around, saw the kindergartners staring at him with awe, and decided not to tell them that Fire Station Number One didn't even have a pole. For two more blocks the little boys talked about washing the fire truck.

Parker pulled into a parking place. Four pairs of eyes spotted the playground. "Can we go play first?" Billy asked.

"We'll have to talk to Mrs. McCoy about that." Parker helped Billy while the rest of the boys scrambled past him. One towheaded imp actually took three steps in the wrong direction before Parker was able to grasp a back belt loop and tug the child in the right direction.

"Welcome to Mayhill Library." Izzy grinned easily, her eyes wandering over the expressions on the children's faces.

She gave Rhea a quick hug and turned to nod at the parent drivers. Her brows went up when she saw Parker.

"These are all kindergartners," Rhea explained, distracting Izzy. "They will be learning their sounds this year, and a few of them will take the big step into reading. They're excited about coming here today.

"You know Tonya. Have you met my brother?"

"Yes, just one week ago." Izzy forced a tight smile at the man.

Parker enjoyed watching her squirm. "And I'm still just dandy."

"Yes. Well. . ." Izzy shrugged before addressing the schoolchildren. "Follow me. This is the children's section. Whiskers, our rabbit, has been looking forward to your visit. He counted the books last night and wants you to know our library has over 15,000 books. Some have only pictures, and others have only words."

The children looked aghast at the thought of a book not having pictures. Parker followed as Izzy led them down the aisle with books suitable for small hands and curious browsing. He watched her gather the children into a circle and show them the three books she planned to share. All the adults, including his sister, vanished. He felt uncomfortable as if he should leave too, but he didn't. Just wait until he got hold of his sister. She'd probably arranged for Delta to cancel.

Parker sat on an undersized chair, knees nearly to his chin, and watched. It was harder than he'd anticipated. Her white dress, with the bold red flowers, moved invitingly every time she turned the page of the book. When she kicked off her sandals halfway through the second book, Parker found that he couldn't take his eyes off her ankles. He was too old for this. He'd married at twenty-two, became a widower at twenty-six, moved to the big city at twenty-seven, returned home at twenty-eight, and now the thought of tempting fate and falling in love again felt like too much of a chance. Being a fireman gave him enough excitement. He didn't need the worry of a woman, and he could tell by the upswept hairstyle of Isobelle de la Rosa that she wasn't one to stay home in the evening. She'd want to go to plays in Lincoln, eat dinner in town at least once a week, and probably try to attend all the town meetings. She'd. . .probably drive too fast in the snow.

At the end of the third story, he glanced around searching for his sister. He located her leaning against the checkout desk holding a few paperbacks to her chest and laughing quietly with Tonya Summer. Behind him, Izzy urged each child to find two books to take home. Rhea walked up, calling her class to attention. Library cards were passed around, books were checked out, and the visit ended.

Four little boys surrounded him, handing Parker their books, and shifting from foot to foot. Parker recognized the movement. He steered them toward the rest room, wishing for assistance but finding none. He held the books while the children tarried. Finally, Parker exited the library with a sigh of relief, pushing the little boys ahead of him. Billy turned around. "I hafta go to the bathroom."

"You just went." Parker looked back at the library with dismay. He did not want to go back in.

"I only went a little."

"I'll watch the others. You take him in." Rhea smiled encouragingly. "We've decided to let the children play for a while."

With a whoop, the kindergartners raced for the monkey bars. Billy looked uncertainly after his friends and then back at the library where the bathroom waited. "I gotta hurry!"

Izzy sat behind the desk, head bent as she sorted through the applications for library cards that Rhea's class had just turned in. She looked up when Parker and Billy entered. "Lose something?"

"Just need to use the facilities." He hurried Billy to the back, leaning outside the door and waiting impatiently.

"How are you doing today?" She was right beside him, her voice falling gently on his ear, sounding too comforting. He hadn't even heard her coming.

"I'm just dandy."

"You keep saying that."

"I was doing dandy the last time we talked, too."

She fidgeted with the sleeve to her dress, rolling it up and then pushing it back down. "This is a nice town. I like it here."

"Billy." Parker knocked on the door, needing to distract himself from her perfume. "Hurry up."

"I just remembered that Mama told me I had to say the ABCs before finishing," Billy hollered.

"What letter are you on?" Parker said, hoping the boy was on the letter U.

"You made me forget, so now I gotta start over."

Parker turned to look at Izzy, frowning down at the woman who stood a full foot shorter than him. "Don't you have something you need to be doing?" The words came out gruffer than he'd intended.

Izzy didn't blink at his tone, instead her eyes seemed to say she understood. "I'm supposed to make sure everyone who comes to the library has the assistance they need. Can I help you find anything?"

"No." He stared, hard, trying to convince her—and himself—that she wasn't needed.

"What do you do in this town for fun?"

Billy chose that moment to come through the bathroom door. Parker bent, grateful for the timely interruption and snapped the boy's pants shut. "I work."

❧

"He works." Izzy mumbled to herself, adding the names of the children to the computer. A few of them had library cards. Izzy made note of those names, determined to drop a postcard to the parents telling them how much the library enjoyed their patronage. The students who were new to the system received a "Welcome to the Library" package.

Parker hadn't smiled when he picked up that child. Imagine holding a sticky-fingered imp and not enjoying the wiggling motion. The poor man. Izzy didn't think Parker realized how much he was missing by hiding behind the facade of pain. She had driven by the fire station twice since last Tuesday, but she'd hoped not to run into him—in person—again so soon. After watching him in the library, she knew the attraction she felt wasn't just because of the alarming paragraph she'd inadvertently read, but the man himself.

"He works." Two proofs of address slipped through her fingers and swirled to the floor. Izzy bent down to retrieve them.

"Who works?" Carole came up behind her.

Izzy smiled, but didn't answer.

Carole smirked knowingly. "Did you have fun with the kiddos?"

"Of course. Did you have fun at the doctor?"

"Er, can you believe it? I waited a half hour and never got to see him. Some sort of emergency came up. I'll bet Tonya Summers came along with her little girl."

"Uh-huh," Izzy nodded.

"Did Delta McKenna help out?"

"No. Didn't see her."

"Well, tell me about your afternoon!"

"I helped fifteen children pick out thirty books. The poor rabbit got poked by numerous fingers. Your husband called to tell you he got the tickets to the play you wanted to see in Lincoln. He seemed really surprised to find out you had a doctor's appointment."

"Guess I forgot to mention it to him." Carole stuck her purse under the counter and headed back for the coffeepot.

Izzy could hear Carole's laughter escaping as she tried to pour herself a cup. *Great*, thought Izzy, realizing she'd been the victim of a setup. *Just great! Carole's pushing me at Parker because she thinks we're a match made in heaven, and I'm practically throwing myself at him because I'm afraid if somebody doesn't start paying attention to him he'll have a nervous breakdown or something.* It was the "or something" that had her worried.

She pushed aside lingering thoughts of Parker Strickland

and concentrated on catching up on some of the more pressing matters.

It was after seven when she got home. Radar had left tufts of hair by the front door. Izzy picked them up and threw them away, washing her hands at the sink. Scooping the cat up, she nuzzled him under her chin. "Are you hungry?"

A disgusting slab of liver lay shriveled in his dish. Izzy deposited the cat back onto the floor and dumped the liver in the toilet and flushed. Radar meowed piteously, chagrined that the treat had slipped by him. Izzy poured hot water in the sink to soak the dried-up liver resin from the dish. "Liver. Ugh, I hate liver."

20

The McKennas' rooster woke Parker, and he wished the bird would develop fowl laryngitis. He'd left the school yesterday a jumbling mass of nerves and driven for miles into the countryside trying to organize his feelings. Some of the farmhouses he'd passed had been the caches for Julia's furnishing quest. She'd been so intent on filling the house with antiques. Izzy didn't look as if she'd care for old sewing machines and hall trees. More likely her domain featured contemporary white and track lights. No matter how many stubbled wheat fields he sped by, he'd been unable to drive thoughts of the librarian from his mind. He'd returned home after midnight, falling on the sofa, glad that he'd awake to a double shift.

It only took twenty minutes to get to work. Parker's great-great-grandfather, Darby Mayhill, had helped build the fire station. Pictures of old volunteers and employees smiled from gray frames. When his father was young, the fire station had been manned strictly by volunteers. Mayhill had experienced a growth spurt during the seventies, thanks to fast food chains desiring prime locations near the interstate. Now working alongside the sheriff and his posse of volunteers were four full-time employees. Robert Parrish served as chief, and Tyler had signed on as an engineer. Jeff worked as captain. Parker was the paramedic. His usual shift was twenty-four hours on, twenty-four hours off with every other weekend free. Ty was attending a workshop in Lincoln, and Parker had volunteered to cover his shift. It was just as easy to sleep in the fire station's cubicle as it was to sleep on a sofa in a lonely living room.

Parker made a notation in the logbook, stating that the school's request had been unfulfilled due to unexpected parental interference. He would explain to Robert and see if the chief wanted a more detailed report.

He'd eaten lunch at Summers, wishing Izzy would walk in, sit across from him, and ask if he were okay. Why did it seem so important to her how he felt? The fire station remained calm all afternoon. Reruns played on the television while Jeff drank coffee and worked on updating the files. Parker went in the back and lifted weights until it was time for supper. Just as the firemen picked up their forks to eat, the phone rang.

≈

"What do you mean you've been trying to get him down all afternoon? How did he get up there?" Izzy tried not to sound upset. The old man was excited enough for both of them.

"I didn't let him out. It was a plain, ordinary day. I went to the library, read the paper, my usual thing. When I came home, I happened to hear him meowing up there. I called him, but he wouldn't come down, then I went in and cooked some liver, thinking to entice him."

"Radar," Izzy called, stepping closer to the tree and peering up through the branches. Radar was a dark silhouette. Izzy put one hand to the tree, thinking to climb up.

"This is an old tree, Izzy. Some of those branches probably wouldn't hold you."

The dark branches waved at her, daring her to climb up. That, combined with her fear of heights, stopped her. "I'll go call Carole. She'll get Jake to bring over his ladder and get Radar down."

"Ah, Izzy." Whip looked at the ground. "I already called the fire department."

Whip's words were still hanging in the air as the fire truck came around the corner and halted in front of the house. Almost in one accord, the neighbors peeked out doorways and windows before moseying over to stand on the sidewalk in case advice was needed.

"Is there a fire?"

"What's all the commotion?"

"Hey, Parker, you really need the truck just to rescue a cat?"

"It's no fun without the engine," Robert joked, shooing the spectators back.

Parker eyed the tree, and Izzy could tell he was considering the dimensions and wondering how he'd get that cat down while maintaining his dignity.

"What do you feed that thing?" Parker frowned.

Whip saved her from answering. "I've been cooking him liver at least twice a week."

"Look, Mr. Strickland," Izzy spoke up. "I didn't call you, and I'm sorry that we've disturbed your evening. I'm sure Radar will get down. Why don't you—"

Whip interrupted, "Izzy! What are you saying? Radar is an indoor cat. What if he decided to come down in the middle of the night? He could get lost." Whip turned to Parker. "You can't leave him up there."

Izzy opened her mouth to protest. Parker glanced over at Robert. Izzy waited for the captain to intercede and make a decision, maybe even take over. But Robert looked to be enjoying the spectacle.

A drop of rain hit Parker on the nose. The fireman squinted, looking up the tree as a few more drops splattered across his forehead. Exasperated, he grumbled, "Radar, you named your cat Radar? Can't you call him and get him to come down?"

Izzy smiled haughtily and looked up, calling sweetly, "Radar."

Meow, came the answer.

"Come down here," Izzy ordered.

Meow, meow.

"He says he won't come down." Izzy crossed her arms and glared at Parker. "My cat has a mind of his own."

"I ought to just leave him up there," Parker muttered.

"That's fine with me. He'll come down when he's ready. I doubt if he'd let you get hold of him, anyway."

"I've rescued plenty of cats from trees."

"My cat doesn't need rescuing. He'll be fine."

"Izzy," Whip interrupted. "It's going to pour any minute."

"Whip, if it rains, the cat will come down. No problem."

"Why don't we just set a dish of food down. He'll come, if he smells something to eat." Parker looked at Whip. "You have any of that liver left?"

Izzy said, "Radar is a cat, not a dog, Mr. Strickland. You can't trick him with food."

"I take it you think cats are superior?" Parker challenged.

The look she shot him let him know she did.

It also inspired him to retort, "As an experienced firefighter I can attest that I've never been called to rescue a dog from a tree."

"Yes, well, those who are afraid to risk adventure seldom find any excitement in life."

"Are you saying dogs are passive?"

"No, actually I was thinking of you."

Silence surrounded them. All the neighbors waited for the next sentence. Robert pushed away from the truck and stepped closer to listen.

Parker reached up to grasp the lowest branch of the tree, ignoring the rain. As he hoisted himself up, he looked one last time at Izzy.

Izzy stood on the ground seething. She hoped Radar bit him. She hoped. . . .

"Got him!" came a cocky yell.

Radar didn't look happy coming down the tree in Parker's arms. The fireman held his victim firmly, since the cat seemed bound and determined to stay at the top. Parker's attempts to hold the animal reminded Izzy of something from a B movie. By the time Parker jumped to the ground, he had a long scratch on his cheek and a furious feline tucked under his arm while his other hand held a fistful of fur. He handed cat and fur to Izzy.

Whip clucked sympathetically, patting Parker on the back. "Come on in, my boy. I'll doctor those scratches, and then you and Robert can sit down for a slice of my peach pie."

"You didn't do much to earn your piece of pie," Parker complained to Robert as they followed the old man inside.

Izzy stroked her cat. "You've upset Radar," she accused.

"I wouldn't have missed this evening for anything," Robert chuckled.

Whip pulled out a chair at the table and urged Robert into it, while directing Parker toward the back bathroom where the bandages awaited. Izzy sat her cat down on the floor and stomped upstairs.

Behind her, Whip chuckled. "That cat's claws are very sharp. Let me put something on those scratches."

She heard Parker mutter, "I'm all right."

❧

Parker sighed and followed the old man down the hall.

Whip fumbled with Mercurochrome. "She sure sets store by that cat. I'll bet you're a hero in her eyes. She's a nice girl."

Great, thought Parker, *first my sister and now Whip Thompson.* The whole town seemed to be in on some diabolical plan to coerce him and Isobelle de la Rosa into couplehood.

Whip finished and beckoned Parker to follow him back into the kitchen. Robert sat in front of his empty plate, bliss written across his face, crumbs decorating his mustache. "You have to taste this pie."

Parker knew how good Whip's pies were. He'd spent many a Saturday afternoon in this kitchen as a boy, with Thelma Thompson stuffing him with pies after he had mown their yard. That's what he'd charged back then. Two dollars and a piece of pie.

"Izzy!" Whip went to the stairs and hollered.

"What?" Her voice tumbled down into the kitchen.

Parker noticed Robert's face contorting with a smirk. Good grief, could it be that his boss was in on it too? And yesterday at the station Jeff had wanted to come along to the school and watch Parker with the children. It was suddenly all too clear. Rhea had never intended to have him teach the children to "Stop, Drop, and Roll." She'd planned on tricking him into going to the library right from the beginning. He had to admire how fast his friends had put that plan together.

"Come on down for some pie!" Whip called up the stairs.

"I don't want any, thanks."

Parker smiled, knowing he was the reason she didn't want any. It felt good, being one up on her for the first time. He dug in, savoring the peachy goodness.

Robert cleared his throat. "We need to be going."

Taking one last bite, Parker wiped his mouth with a napkin. He stood, holding out his hand for Whip to shake. After that was done, he walked over to the stairs. "Miss de la Rosa," he called.

"What?" Impatience oozed from the word.

"If my dog ever gets stuck in a tree, I'll be sure to call you."

Robert pushed him out the door, whispering, "You don't have a dog."

"She doesn't know that."

❧

The puppy woke Parker up. Its lumpy paws were more effective than McKennas' rooster. "Down, Brute."

He'd gotten the puppy yesterday, taking his day off and answering an ad he'd found in the paper. The more he'd thought, the more he'd wondered why he didn't want Izzy to find out that he'd lied to her.

The dog had spent the drive home howling or burying its wet nose on the side of Parker's neck while flopping puppy paws raked at the leather seat. A few times the puppy had climbed into the extended cab, as if looking for something. Parker had winced, but let the puppy whimper. Maybe the dog was lamenting the fading scent of his mother or possibly the motion of the car upset his stomach.

Parker rubbed Brute's head, thinking of the way the puppy's mother had followed her offspring all the way to his truck and how the ancient farmer had told him not to worry, that the dog was a good-natured mutt.

The farmer had spit on the ground and advised, "He'll be a big dog. Just look at his paws. Lots of Golden Retriever in his bloodline."

Lying on the couch, Parker watched the puppy snuggle closer. He reached over and laid his hand on the puppy's head and tickled Brute behind the ears, then he kicked back the covers and threw his feet over the edge of the couch. Brute jumped down and scampered to the door, whimpering to go out.

"I don't think so," Parker said. Yesterday, when they'd pulled up in front of the farmhouse, Parker had made the mistake of letting the puppy jump from the car on its own, and as a consequence had spent the next two hours trying to get Brute to come out from under the porch.

Parker had finally crawled under the wooden lattice, amid the dirt and scurrying bugs, and dragged Brute out by one paw. He didn't intend to tell Izzy about the experience, because it had taken far longer to retrieve Brute than it had to rescue Radar. And there was no pie after.

Brute had been a mess, too. His blond mongrel hair stood in clumps. Twigs and grass stuck in his whiskers. Parker plopped Brute into the kitchen sink and turned the faucet on. Afterwards, he took the squirming puppy out into the yard, attached the collar to a long rope, and went back inside. For all of twenty minutes.

He hoped the noise also disturbed the rooster. He decided a trip to the library was necessary, to look up the information. Maybe he'd even have to ask a certain librarian for help, and of course he'd mention the joy of having a puppy. The puppy who didn't like being tied up outside.

The puppy that had shared Parker's couch.

four

"Yes, Izzy, this is Jake Martin." The mayor's voice boomed over the phone line, excitement accentuated in each word. "I've got a two o'clock appointment scheduled with Mark Dalton of the *Mayhill Daily*. Fred Rasmussen will also be there. Can you come? We're going to discuss next year's celebration of Founding Day. Do you realize that Mayhill's first settlers stopped their wagons on this spot roughly one hundred years ago?"

"How could I *not* know?" Izzy laughed. Jake had started promoting the centennial last January. Already storefronts displayed pioneers holding shovels with banners that proclaimed, "Mayhill or Bust."

She flipped open her planner and stared at her schedule. Thursday. It had been a week since Parker Strickland had rescued her cat. She had seen him around town a few times, or at least she'd seen his truck. Last Sunday she had gone to church and had written Parker's name on a prayer card. Funny how every time she added a commitment to her planner, she thought of Parker.

"Okay, Jake, I can make it this afternoon." The only unusual venture planned for today was a three-thirty appointment with a high school girl about part-time employment. Carole could do the interview if Izzy didn't get back in time.

Izzy pushed aside a pile of flyers announcing extended library hours every Tuesday and located last Friday's paper. Mark Dalton dominated the front page with stories of Mayhill's past glories. She scanned the writing, smiling at the mention of a reported sighting of Jesse James by one Margaret Summer. From the arrest of a Nazi criminal to the smiling photo of Greta McKenna representing Big Red in a Miss

America pageant, Mayhill proved it had done its part promoting the pride of Nebraska.

Izzy felt a spark of loyalty. She hadn't been born in this state, but in many ways she felt at home here. Her mother had never been happier.

❧

"They're waiting for you." Agnes Hepfield said.

Izzy smiled. Agnes looked so prim and proper behind the huge cherrywood desk. She'd volunteered to be a secretary on the two days Jake worked at the courthouse. The elderly woman had been his full-time secretary at Martin's Insurance Firm until she'd retired.

Mayhill Courthouse resided right across the street from the library and displayed its history gallantly, from the etched date of 1911 that existed above the door frame to the chipped white pavilion where James McKenna and his band played jazz every Saturday night during the summer.

Jake Martin's office was awash with blue marble. The shiny floor looked like a museum's. A painting of George Washington gazed with dignity over the furnishings. Izzy found herself scrutinizing the signature, almost expecting to see an autograph by the first president himself.

Jake leaned back in a leather chair, hands folded sternly in front of him. Mark Dalton scribbled in his notebook and didn't bother looking up at her entrance. Fred Rasmussen wheezed from the corner where he was getting a drink from a distilled water cooler.

"Glad you could make it." Jake rose from the chair, arm stretched out in greeting, pure politician stance.

Mark nodded, quit writing, and looked up. "I'll be glad to turn over copies of the old *Daily*s when you begin research and—"

"Do you think I could have a cigarette?" Fred interrupted.

"Don't worry," Jake said, seeing Izzy's distressed look. "His daughter made him quit. Now all he does is chew on them."

"Women," Fred complained.

"Izzy." Jake cleared his throat. "Mark jumped the gun a bit. We called you here because I, er, Mark had the bright idea of doing a biography of Rosemary Mayhill's life. We thought that since you've done such a good job of refurbishing the library, you might like to be in charge of writing up her history. What do you think?"

"A better woman never lived." Fred Rasmussen feebly sat down in the seat next to Izzy's.

"What kind of history?" Izzy tried to pretend she wasn't interested. She knew the talk of politics. She didn't like it, but she knew it. Truthfully, the thought of being commissioned to research the finer points surrounding the first librarian of Mayhill intrigued Izzy. Rosemary Mayhill had been years ahead of her time. The cornerstone of both the town and the church.

"We were thinking that we'd focus in on at least five past citizens and expound on their good works for the community. Sort of a 'they made a difference' topic. Rosemary Mayhill and Alias Summer were voted as unanimous choices. Mark thinks you'd be perfect as the writer of Mrs. Mayhill's mini-biography. He's going to do Alias's."

Mark nodded. "During the Saturday-evening celebration, we'll role play the parts of the forefounders."

"What do you think?" Jake leaned forward eagerly. The light in his eyes told Izzy he was sure that this event would help keep him mayor for years after the spectacle.

"Sounds like a lot of work," Izzy said.

"You could work on it during business hours." Jake smiled.

Izzy opened her purse and took out her planner, slowly opening the book and studying her schedule with a pretend scowl. "I'm only going to be here four more months, and with Carole gone, I'll be very busy at the library. Now that school's started again, I've got lots of students needing help, plus with the onset of winter, patrons check out a large number of books, anticipating being inside during blizzards."

"I'm waiting for you to order that new book by that fancy New York lawyer," Fred spoke up. "Be sure you get it in large print."

Mark settled back in his chair, watching Izzy with an interested expression.

"Mayor Martin, my time is very valuable." Izzy leaned forward, looking at Jake Martin with raised eyebrows. "The task is extremely appealing, but I may have to pass. Oh, by the way, when do the city commissioners plan on finalizing next year's budget?"

Jake picked up a pen and tapped it against his desk calendar.

"That's all been decided," Mark began and then choked.

"Some decisions have already been made." Jake started examining his hand with intent interest.

"Just how thoroughly did you discuss my motion for three computers to be installed for patron use at the library?"

"We haven't made any firm decisions about monies allotted to the library yet."

Izzy stood, sticking her planner back in her purse and smiling at Jake. "I originally requested five, you know."

"Three seems like a reasonable number," Jake responded.

"How long do you want the report on Rosemary Mayhill to be?"

"You can go over the details with Mark." Jake came around the desk and shook Izzy's hand. "He'll be in charge of the final program."

"Let's get Fred over to his apartment, Izzy. I'll fill you in on my ideas, and maybe you can make some suggestions." Mark stuck his notecards in his pocket and helped Fred stand.

The retirement home squatted two buildings down from the city hall. With a young person on each side, Fred slowly made his way outside. "When I was born, only five thousand people lived in Mayhill. It was pure farm country then, had just one restaurant and that was run by the Summers family as an offshoot of the store."

Mark and Izzy smiled at each other over the bent gray

head, and then Mark cleared his throat before loudly saying, "Fred, how'd you like to meet Izzy and me for dinner tomorrow night?"

"Excuse me," Izzy frowned, "tomorrow night I—"

"Will certainly want to meet with Fred to ask him questions about Rosemary Mayhill," Mark finished her sentence.

Fred took two steps up the retirement center's walk. "You young people let me know if your argument ends with a yes to dinner."

"We'll pick you up at seven," Mark said.

"We'll let you know," Izzy butted in.

Fred waved good-bye, chuckling advice. "Take charge, my boy."

"I could be busy tomorrow night," Izzy said, turning toward the library.

"It's not your bowling night. You never go to Summers'. Your parents are in Florida. I think you're available."

Izzy sputtered indignantly, "Why you snoop! How do you know all that? What gives you the right—?"

Mark laughed and easily threw his arm around her shoulders companionably. "Welcome to small-town America. There's not much to be known. I bowl on Tuesday nights and always check the boards to compare high scores. You're a good bowler, by the way. Carole's been a friend of my family's for years. She likes to talk, so I know all about the things you do for fun. I hear you're getting pretty good at crocheting dishcloths. As for your parents still being in Florida, I'm a reporter, Izzy. I'm supposed to snoop. Now, what about dinner? Fred Rasmussen will be the perfect chaperone."

❧

Parker sat in his truck watching Izzy with dismay. What was she doing with that weasel, Mark Dalton? It was almost too much to bear when Dalton threw his arm around Izzy's shoulders. In Parker's opinion, Mark rated just a little bit above Kenny.

Parker sighed. It was probably for the best. He didn't want

to be interested in Izzy, anyway. Now that he knew she was seeing Mark Dalton, Parker would just stay away from the library. He had a new puppy for companionship. He didn't need or want a woman, especially not one who wanted him to give his time to a Bible study. He knew the Bible. His parents occasionally attended services. He refused to be a hypocrite: living one way; feeling another.

The puppy yawned in agreement. Parker petted the top of the dog's head and started the engine. He'd go visit his folks and then head home.

❧

The minute Mark got into the car, leaving Izzy free to return to the library, she let out a silent whoop. She'd been planning on researching the woman's life on her own. There were many magazines interested in publishing the stories concerning pioneer women and to think that she could use working hours to get the job done.

"Well, did Jake talk you into it?" Carole handed books back to a patron and smiled at Izzy.

"He certainly did."

"And how many computers did he agree to?"

"What! How? Oh, Carole, you're a charmer. How did you know I'd use those computers as leverage?"

"Because you're a smart girl. I hear Parker rescued your cat last week."

"Hurrumph."

Carole wagged a finger. "I know Mark Dalton is not the right man for you."

"Guess what? I know that too."

"Good," Carole teased. "I'd hate to think of your settling for Mark Dalton when Parker Strickland's a possibility."

A loud sneeze echoed off the library's walls. Carole and Izzy glanced over to where Whip was exiting his chair. "Parker's a good man," Thompson said. "He has great taste in pies." He headed for the door, throwing back over his shoulder. "And women."

Izzy felt embarrassment steal up her cheeks. She forced herself to remain calm. "Carole, if you don't leave my love life alone, I will go out with Mark Dalton."

Carole wasn't fooled. "I doubt that."

"Mark's a fine man. An excellent journalist. A fine judge of bowling scores. We share many like interests."

"Mark has a girlfriend in Lincoln. Seems to think he's fair game until the wedding day, which is in June. Parker is more reliable."

"He's impossible," Izzy muttered.

"He's what?"

"Nothing. And, it doesn't matter anyway. I'm moving back to Phoenix soon. Don't you have work to do?"

Carole grinned and began emptying the drop box. "Sure, and so do you. Oh, Delta McKenna wants you to call her."

Izzy stepped behind the front desk and helped a patron who suddenly appeared from behind the biography section.

Carole returned to the desk, and Izzy went into the office. It seemed as if she was getting less and less of her own work completed. Unless she took matters in hand, and quickly, she'd have little time to work on Rosemary's life.

A stack of messages waited atop her computer. Two were personal, and she dispensed of them quickly. One was a thank-you from Jake Martin, and the last was from Delta McKenna. Izzy took a breath and dialed Delta's number. Delta probably wanted to do a movie or something. She had lived in Mayhill all her life. She'd turned up pregnant during her senior year of high school and refused to tell who the father was. Most of the bowling league women seemed to think it was a boy from Waco named Chris Walker. Izzy remembered that Agatha had said Chris was Kenny's cousin. That would make Chris a relative of Parker's too. Parker's roots sank deep in Mayhill history.

Others claimed the father was Carole's boy, Tom. Carole denied that and said it was probably Chris, but that Delta had dated anyone who walked. Whip said it was nobody's business.

Izzy agreed, and was proud of the way Delta held her head high and dared anyone to look down on her or her boy. She'd begun attending church again merely a month ago. Her Christianity was fragile. Izzy sometimes sat next to her during services. Delta struggled, that Izzy could see. The old life called, and commitment was still divided.

"Thanks for returning my call so quickly," Delta said. "Dad wants to attend the gun show in Lincoln Friday night. Mom and I thought we'd get some shopping done. Would you be willing to stay with Billy for the weekend?"

"I really—" Izzy tried.

"I know how last minute this is and how busy you are, and normally I wouldn't think to bother you, but Bushy is about to have her first batch of kittens. The vet says it will most likely be this weekend, and Billy so wants to be here. I just know if we leave, Bushy will give birth, and Billy will be devastated."

"Well, I—"

"We'll be glad to pay you."

"Delta, that's not it. I have plans for tomorrow night and—"

"Of course. I'm sure Bushy will be fine, and Billy can be there the next time. Dad was planning on getting the cat fixed, but perhaps I can convince him—"

"I'll be glad to do it." Izzy knew when to give in.

"I'll drop the keys by the library this afternoon. Tomorrow, Billy will walk to the library instead of taking the bus home. I can't tell you how much we appreciate this."

Izzy hung up the phone, feeling drained. Jake Martin better beware. If Delta McKenna ever took a mind to run for Congress, he wouldn't have a chance against her if it came to bargaining.

❧

Billy obediently sat in the children's section and looked at a picture book.

Izzy kept a sharp eye on him, checking to make sure he was behaving. He stayed close to the rabbit. Maybe the kid would be a veterinarian when he grew up. Suddenly, Izzy began looking forward to the evening. Mark had agreed to pick up Fred and bring him out to the McKennas' farm. Izzy would purchase plenty of food at the grocery store and intended to make a four-course meal. She rarely got the opportunity to cook, and she wanted to go all out. She'd worked her way through college via the restaurant route. She'd waitressed, cooked, bussed, and even managed. Sharing a kitchen with Whip had curtailed her culinary daring. Besides, with the old man cooking, she'd already put on eight pounds since she'd moved in.

"Are you ready?" she asked Billy after making sure Carole knew she was leaving.

"Yep," Billy lisped toothlessly, digging in his back pocket and extracting a wrinkled piece of paper. "Mom said you hadn't been ta the house before so she drew ya a map."

Izzy took the damp piece of paper, wondering where the wetness came from, yet glad she didn't know. Delta had drawn a detailed route to the McKenna farm.___

"You live," Izzy cleared her throat, suddenly remembering, "behind Parker Strickland's place?"

"Yes, maybe tomorra we kin go over and play with his puppy."

"I don't think so," Izzy managed, turning into the local grocery store's parking lot.

Izzy didn't use the map to find the McKennas' house. Her twilight romp to Parker's house, to collect a made-up library fine, was a vivid memory. The McKennas lived right next door, albeit a quarter-mile down the way. Izzy had turned around in their driveway.

Of course, the place looked different in the fading daylight. It was nestled amid a landscape of green grass and winding driveway. The dirt road shot pebbles from under Izzy's tires as she skidded toward the white garage. An old well stood to the left of the two-story house. The smell of animals and nature hit Izzy full force when she parked her car alongside the barn. Clouds were gathering in the distant skies.

"Park behind the barn," Billy ordered. "You can see my rabbit hutches."

"Have you lived here all your life?" Izzy helped Billy out of the car.

"Yes, Mama made the big mistake when she was seventeen, and we've lived here ever since." Billy took Izzy's hand and led her to a homemade wooden structure.

Izzy knew the big mistake was Delta getting pregnant out of wedlock. From Billy's tone, she didn't think he thought of himself as the big mistake, just of his mama as making one that he was as of yet uncertain about.

After Billy introduced Izzy to seven bunnies, all named after dwarves, he took off running for the front door. Izzy fumbled in her purse for the key, but Billy careened into the house without halting.

They don't lock the door, Izzy said to herself in amazement.

Lights came on in every room as Billy ran through the house. Izzy followed more slowly taking in the layout. She touched a finger to the floral wallpaper of the kitchen and imagined the sense of generation after generation blending together to make what existed now. The very smell of the air tingled with history.

She went back outside and emptied the car of its groceries. Leaving everything on the kitchen counters, she came to the living room and sat down on a large couch. The television looked comfortable next to the obviously homemade brick fireplace. Dark pictures, depicting stern-looking ancestors in black and white, graced the walls.

A glance at the clock put Izzy on her feet again. She had just a few hours to prepare supper for her visitors. Billy entered the kitchen and proudly displayed five favorite stuffed animals while Izzy measure, poured, chopped, and stirred.

Only the sounds of crickets and locusts blanketed the night air around the McKenna farm. Thunder sounded once, then faded to nothingness. Izzy stood on the back porch, wiping a cold hand over her damp brow. The kitchen had warmed up soon after she'd turned on the stove. The smell of lasagna permeated the musty air. The dark sky taunted her with blue and gray clouds that moved threateningly toward the fading moon. The moon hazed in the distance.

Billy tripped out to the porch, carrying a protesting, extremely pregnant cat. "Bushy wants to be near you."

"Let's sit and wait for Mark and Mr. Rasmussen."

"My grandma says Mark Dalton better go home when Mr. Rasmussen does."

From the mouth of babes, Izzy thought. "Don't worry, he will. Put that poor cat down and come inside."

The cat went under the porch. Billy led Izzy inside. She checked the lasagna. Billy pulled a building block game from under the coffee table and set about creating some sort of oddly shaped car. Izzy divided her time between the kitchen and living room.

It was just after seven when headlights glowed from miles away. Izzy knew they belonged to Mark. No one else would be out on a night like this, with a storm threatening to appear, especially on a country road that led nowhere, and Parker's truck sat silhouetted in his driveway, a testament that he was home. The glow danced as the driver hit ruts in the curving road that had once served only wagons.

"I forgot about that road," Mark laughed, stepping out of the car.

Izzy opened Fred's side. The old man's hand sailed through the air as he tried to find a firm foundation to brace himself against. Izzy offered her arm.

"No," he grumbled. "Mark."

Mark came around the car and helped Fred out. "He's not real comfortable with equality, yet." Mark led Fred to the door.

"Delta's grandmama used to have the best barn dances." Fred looked around in admiration. Billy heard the reference to the great-grandmother he'd never met and positioned himself behind Fred's feet, dangerously close to the wavering cane.

"Put Fred at the table," Izzy ordered.

"Don't forget to turn off the stove," Fred advised.

Izzy looked at Mark with alarm. Was there something wrong with the oven? Mark shook his head helplessly.

Once the food hit the table, Fred forgot about the stove and plunged in with a joyous abandonment that awed Izzy. Izzy opened her mouth, then shut it. She didn't want to embarrass the elderly man. Reaching over, she took Billy's hand and whispered a quick prayer of thanks for the meal. Mark stopped eating but didn't join in.

Fred didn't notice at all. No one had ever shown so much appreciation for her food before. He didn't even complain because she'd gone a little liberal with the amount of ketchup she used in the sauce.

Billy turned up his nose at the Italian fare and settled for a peanut butter and jelly sandwich. The continuing thunder kept Izzy on the edge of her seat, smiling brightly, and trying to act as if nothing bothered her.

After the meal, she led everyone into the living room, and they gathered around the coffee table, Mark and Izzy with notebooks in hand, Billy stroking a bloated feline and keeping his building blocks from straying too close to Fred's feet.

Mark began the questions, "Did you know Alias Summer?"

"Not really. . . ."

Two hours later, Fred dropped off in the middle of a sentence. His "not really" reference had expanded into a blow-by-blow account of the many dealings he'd had with the man. His history narration started with his childhood, as a young boy shoveling snow. Later, he detailed the life of a doctor trying to contend with a self-diagnosing patient. They never got around to discussing Rosemary Mayhill.

Izzy fumed silently, trying hard to keep her temper in check. The book of Psalms described the Lord as being slow to anger. Izzy believed the teaching, lived it, but sometimes had a hard time enjoying it. The nerve of Mark, allowing her to cook the meal and then to be forced to listen to an old man discuss only aspects pertaining to Mark's portion of the historical assignment. Every time she'd tried to direct the questions to Rosemary, Mark had smoothly turned the topic back to Alias.

"He's falling asleep, and Billy's been asleep for over an hour," Izzy whispered. "Time for you guys to leave."

Mark grinned, raising an eyebrow in a suggestive pose that Izzy hadn't witnessed since college. The man who attempted to impress her back then hadn't been successful either.

Izzy opened the front door—surely, Mark would take the hint—and stepped out onto the porch. Mark followed, without Fred. She counted to ten, but that didn't help. Sunday school had told her that patience was a virtue, but it continued to be a virtue Izzy lacked.

"Mark," Izzy said, "very few men have irritated me as thoroughly as you have this evening. I can with complete assurance predict that you and I have no future. I think you're a complete jerk." A clap of thunder added emphasis to her words. "And it's time for you to leave."

"I don't understand," Mark pretended.

"You poor thing. I believe you've dated girls who lie to you about your appeal. You know exactly why I'm irritated at you. Next time you want to interview somebody, have your mother do the cooking. I hear crow is especially easy to prepare. Now leave."

Mark came a little closer, amusement and something else dancing in his expression. Izzy frowned as she realized that he hadn't believed a word she'd said. She was too tired to mess with this. Back in Phoenix, the public library had hosted numerous safety seminars. Izzy had attended more than one. A woman had many options to take if she felt threatened. In the middle of nowhere, on an almost stormy Friday night, Izzy wished she had a whistle or can of mace. Not that Mark deserved that, but. . .

She'd first utilized her screaming skills in the backyard of her Arizona home at age eight. Playing in the desert had been fun. With her friends, she'd chased lizards and dug holes. She and her two best friends happened upon a little snake while following the exploits of a roadrunner. Anna had screamed first, but no one noticed, so Izzy had taken a deep breath and let loose a sound that summoned three sets of parents.

The last time Izzy screamed had been at the Phoenix Library when one of her mother's friends had came for her. . . to tell her that her father had. . .to tell her. . .that her father was dead. That scream had been so heart-rending that no one had even given the automatic "shhh." Izzy had done a lot of screaming the week her father had died. Then she'd stopped, until tonight.

Mark's hand on her shoulder released her from her thoughts. She tilted her head back and screamed. Mark jumped. Billy started crying, clearly frightened by what he'd heard. Fred didn't move.

"Izzy," Mark grumbled as he backed away, "you'd think I was going to hurt you."

"You did hurt me," Izzy ground out. "You hurt my feelings and my dignity. I'll definitely add you to my prayers, but I don't think we need to work together anymore."

"Fine by me. I'll send you written guidelines about what to do. You need to stop being so uptight. I thought you'd be grateful for a little excitement. Mayhill must be pretty dreary after Phoenix."

"Grateful? When I meet your girlfriend from Lincoln I'll ask her how grateful she is."

Mark went rigid and stiffly reentered the living room. "Come on, Fred." He shook the old man's shoulder and then hurried the dazed older man out the door.

The rain started as they drove away. Even in the uneven mist, Izzy could see the lights going on one by one at Parker Strickland's farm.

five

Parker heard the truck drive away from McKennas' place. Unless he was mistaken, Mark Dalton had just spent the evening at his neighbors. That didn't explain the scream. If there had been more than one holler, Parker would have rushed over. As it was, the screaming stopped right before Mark left.

Still, something didn't feel quite right. The scream hadn't sounded like Delta or her mom, and her dad certainly wasn't one to shout. Parker paced for a few moments before deciding he'd take a walk in the McKennas' direction, make sure everything looked all right.

Brute tumbled at his feet. In the back of his mind, Parker considered leaving the puppy shut inside, but the dog loved being outdoors. Brute had quickly figured out how to work Parker. A short whine and every wish was appeased. Brute no longer missed his mother. Parker fulfilled his every need.

The night seemed to grow darker as Parker crossed through overgrown fields. It had been seven years since any crops had been planted, and according to his dad, now would be a good time to put his land to use. Parker had no intention of becoming a farmer. He just liked the farmhouse and the privacy of many acres between him and the city.

Rain pelted his face, and Parker almost turned around, went back home. Nothing looked amiss.

He saw the woman on the porch and stopped short. It sure wasn't Delta or her mom sitting there. Besides, Delta usually had a date on Friday night. His gut let him know who it was before he even recognized the long, dark hair and athletic body. What was she doing here?

Thunder crashed and lightning appeared to make the moment look as day. He watched Izzy sitting on the porch, arms tightly wrapped around her own body, and realized she was frightened. All of Parker's instincts told him to go comfort her. He wouldn't. She'd obviously survived thunderstorms without him. She was already in his thoughts more than he wanted her to be. Parker turned, took two steps, paused, pivoted around. Brute made up Parker's mind for him. The small bundle of fur ran ahead, then jumped up and pounced on Izzy's knees.

A sense of foreboding came over him. Brute had wiggled, muddy-pawed, into Izzy's lap and planted a sloppy kiss right on Izzy's chin.

"Are you coming up, Parker?" Izzy's voice clashed with a streak of thunder. She held Brute in her lap and crossed her feet at her ankles.

"Storms scare you?" He stepped out of the shadows.

"A little," she said. "This your dog?"

The wooden slats of the porch creaked under his feet. He looked around, but the only place to sit was alongside Izzy on the porch swing. He settled for the top step, stretching his legs out and wishing she didn't make him long for things he couldn't have. "I heard a scream."

"That was me."

"What did Mark do?"

"He made me mad."

"And so you screamed?" He shifted, sitting Indian style and trying to figure out the truth behind her flippant answers.

"A trick I learned in a defense class. It worked, didn't it? He's gone."

"Who was with him?"

"You're full of questions tonight."

Parker felt his face growing red. The careless splattering of rain turned into a downpour at that moment, saving him from obvious embarrassment. "I'm the only neighbor who came to investigate," he pointed out. "I think that gives me the right to ask a few questions."

"You are the only neighbor," she pointed out. A healthy burst of thunder inspired Brute to bury his nose in Izzy's hand. Izzy stared off in the distance, watching the lightning and chewing her bottom lip.

Parker kept watching her, wondering why she was interested in Mark Dalton and how she'd wound up here at the McKennas' place.

❧

Any other man would have settled down beside her in the porch swing, not Parker. He preferred to sit on the porch with his feet in the mud. Still, she was grateful that he was here. Dark places with thunder-and-lightning sound effects had never been her favorite locations. She wanted him to stay because his presence made her feel safe, and she wanted him to stay because his haunted eyes seemed to cry out for her.

"Let's go in," she heard herself say.

Parker cleared his throat, "Maybe I should—"

"It's dark, it's raining, and your dog's asleep."

Brute had burrowed his way under the porch swing and between two potted plants. Puppy snores added music to the night sounds.

"What's his name?"

"What? Oh, his name is Brute."

"You named a golden retriever Brute?"

"So?"

Izzy tried not to chuckle. "It just doesn't fit."

"Well, I'm not quite sure how your cat came about the name Radar, but I didn't mention that as I extracted him from the tree."

Izzy smiled, glad that Parker was touchy. It was a good sign. "I'll bet the McKennas have Monopoly," Izzy suggested.

Parker stood, slipping out of his muddy boots and nodding. Izzy led the way inside, formulating all the questions she could ask him about his late wife, and about why he always seemed so sad.

While they'd been outside, Billy had come into the living room and laid on the couch. Izzy straightened the blanket over his sleeping form and went to find the game.

"I'll get some candles," Parker called.

Izzy shivered. Candles. What could he. . .?

The lights went out.

In the flashing darkness, Izzy froze. She could hear Parker fumbling and then the striking of a match.

"Izzy?" came a whisper.

"Over here," she whispered back.

The light from the flickering candle found its force, and Izzy turned to see Parker, so silent in his stocking feet, loom up behind her.

"Why are you so frightened of the storm?" he asked.

The shadows from the candle played across his face, highlighting such a serious look that Izzy wanted to touch his chin. She wanted to witness the beginning of a smile change his stoic expression to one of joy.

"Why are you always so sad?" she countered.

He frowned, "I'm not sad. I just don't. . . Listen, we can play Monopoly. It will keep your mind off the storm." He walked into the living room.

Funny, with Parker sitting on the floor across from her, the night didn't seem so scary. The lightning highlighted his hair. The strands were still damp from the heavy rain.

"What piece do you want?" Parker changed the mood from moonlight to reality.

"I'll be the thimble." Izzy handed out the miniatures and located the dice.

His body seemed to take up so much of the living room. Izzy almost felt suffocated, as if his very being demanded her complete attention. She leaned against the sofa while he lounged with his back to the silent television. His eyes were shaded. The stubble on his chin told of his need to shave.

Izzy cleared her throat and started with a safe topic. "So how long have you been a fireman?"

"Almost three years."

Izzy acquired Baltic and St. James Place. "Do you like living in Mayhill?"

He didn't answer until she handed him Park Place. "It's home."

Brute whined from outside. Parker eased his body off the floor and ambled to the door. Izzy watched. The man moved with the ease of a panther. She was getting much too interested. Brute slid in, jumped on the couch, and curled puppy style at Billy's feet.

The clock said midnight. The game had effectively taken her mind off of the storm and now the rain was letting up. Izzy tried to stifle a yawn, and she handed him the last of her money as rent. "Parker, that was a lot of fun."

It looked as if he started to nod, but thought better of it and changed the gesture to a shrug, although he said more in the next sentence than he'd spoken all evening. "I think I'll head home. The storm's mostly over. Let me take Billy upstairs."

Without waiting for an answer, he scooped the little boy up. Izzy felt her heart beat as she watched the man gently rest Billy's head against his shoulder. This was a scene right out of her daydreams. Billy's chin quivered in sleep, and Izzy carefully pushed an errant strand of hair out of Billy's eyes. Parker stared down at her, questions in his eyes.

"You know where his room is?"

"No," Parker whispered.

"Up the stairs, to the left."

The flames from the fireplace shot out an amber of light into the room. Izzy watched the two heads as they bobbed up the stairs. Two reddish-brown heartthrobs. She stood on one foot then another. She'd been with Parker for hours and knew practically nothing about him, except that her quest to save him had doubled. Under his gruff exterior nestled the heart of a teddy bear. If she were to liken him to an apostle, she'd choose Luke, the healer. He didn't like to see people hurting, which was why he hurt so much and probably why he'd put a lock on his heart so he wouldn't chance getting hurt again.

Billy nodded awake before Parker reached the top of the stairs. Izzy heard the muffled words, "You're not Mark."

"Not even close," Parker agreed. After a few minutes, during which time giggles and things dropping echoed down the stairs, Parker came back into the living room, nonchalantly looking around.

"Your boots are on the porch," Izzy said.

She followed him out the door, watching as he sat in the swing to put his boots on.

He stomped away some of the mud that had caked on his boots. Izzy stepped closer. He looked up at the sky and glanced at Izzy warningly. "It's still raining a bit."

She backed away, silently, wanting to appear a shadow.

He hadn't worn a jacket. "I had a nice evening," he murmured, as if it had been a planned meeting.

She nodded mutely. He stood uncertainly and then started across the porch. He hesitated when he got to the steps. Then with a suddenness that left her breathless, he turned, took two big steps in her direction, hooked his hand securely around the base of her neck and brought her mouth to his.

The few drops of rain that shivered on her arms all stood to attention. Izzy felt herself leaning into the kiss, drinking in the taste of him. Her knees brushed against him, and she let her body become enraptured with his as her skin fought to touch him.

Abruptly, he pushed her away. He glared down at her sternly before he turned and marched into the field. Brute followed, dancing excitedly amidst the dripping trees, unaware that his master could accept and return the love of a dog more than he could the possible love of a woman.

હ

Every time his boot sank in the mud, Parker made a fist. What had happened back there? She'd asked more questions than his mother, and he'd fielded all of them. Julia hadn't surfaced even once. So why had he kissed her? She was as innocent as the sky was blue. He should have moved off that porch without looking in her eyes. His boots had already been on, his dog had lain at his feet. There was absolutely no reason for him to turn around, clasp her to his lips, and kiss her. No reason, except that for the first time in years his chest didn't hurt every time he breathed. Except that now the scent of roses put a smile where a smile previously hadn't been welcomed or wanted.

Parker looked up at the skies and wondered what God was up to.

※

Izzy stayed in the office the next day. Every time the door opened, she jumped. Parker's kiss had kept her awake all night. This morning when she had prodded Billy out of bed, he had confided, "My mama likes Parker, too, but she says he's boring."

Then he'd checked his cat, disappointed at nature's delay. On the way to the library, he'd asked all kinds of mindless questions. She'd answered each one patiently, hoping he wouldn't mention Parker anymore. She didn't know if she had the courage to go back to the McKennas'. What if Parker came over again? Worse, what if he didn't?

She took Billy to Summers for lunch. Two of his school friends were there. When it was time to return to work, she gave halting permission for him to play with them at the park in front of the library. She spent the rest of the afternoon working the front desk and watching out the door as Billy and his friends tried to climb the huge, gnarled tree.

"I use to climb that tree when I was in britches." Fred Rasmussen's voice jerked Izzy from her scrutinizing.

Izzy strained to watch as Billy jumped at the limb for the umpteenth time. "He can't quite reach the lowest branch."

"Did you get that book I wanted in large print?"

"Not yet, Mr. Rasmussen." Izzy scooted around on her chair and took the books from Fred's arms. He was one of their better patrons, at least for returning books on time. Something slithered to the floor. Izzy bent, picking up the single page and stared aghast at the paperback book it came from, especially when she noticed that all the pages were loose.

"Mr. Rasmussen, what happened?"

"Arthritis. I can't hold the books comfortably anymore."

Carole walked over, and took the paperback from Izzy's trembling hand. "What did you do?"

"If I tear the pages out. I can hold them more easily."

His cane tapped a Morse code of aged independence as he hobbled to the door.

"What. . .?" Carole began.

Izzy found it far easier to forgive Fred than she had Mark last night. After a quick round of "What would Jesus do?" she said, "We'll see to it he only checks out the books that are beyond repair. He can read them before we dispose of them."

Carole swallowed her laughter and nodded.

When the library closed at six, Izzy grabbed her coat, fed the rabbit, and rushed out the door, barely responding to Carole's good-bye.

"My mama drives this fast," was Billy's only comment as they sped towards the McKenna house.

Izzy checked the speedometer and slowed down.

Parker's house stood empty. Billy supplied the answer. "It's his shift."

Twenty-four on, twenty-four off. There went her plans to invite him to church tomorrow morning.

Saturday evening dragged on, with only the television to offer entertainment, but Sunday came too quickly. She'd learned all sorts of things following Billy around the farm. She'd learned how to gather an egg. It had taken her fifteen minutes to grab the innocent oval from the unthreatening chicken, but she'd done it. She'd climbed an elm tree to investigate Billy's tree-house, made from wood and old John Deere parts.

It almost felt like noon when she pulled into the church's parking lot. Billy trustingly tucked his hand in hers and entered the foyer. She made sure he was safely cocooned in Sunday school and then headed for her own class.

One thing Izzy knew about every church she'd ever attended, and that was: It was hard to be single. Izzy had sat through many a lecture about how to stay a couple. Today was the first time she'd felt vulnerable. As if she'd forgotten to bring something, someone, to church. During all the other "Making the Marriage Work" sermons, she'd dreamed about meeting her future husband. Today, she felt almost ill. The smiling couples, sitting on gray folding chairs, and nodding at the minister's words, had they always known they were meant to be together? Had God directed them toward each other, and when their eyes met had they known? What if she'd met the man God had chosen for her and somehow not recognized him? What if there were no significant other for her?

Izzy wished her mother weren't in Florida. She could sure use some advice, and she wasn't sure she could find the Scripture that pertained to Parker Strickland.

Delta McKenna and her parents pulled into the driveway late Sunday afternoon. Izzy and Billy were watching cartoons on the television. Billy eagerly jumped up and ran outside to leap into his grandpa's arms. Delta's father nodded curtly at Izzy. "Did the cat have the kittens?" the man demanded in a gravelly voice.

"No, Grandpa." Billy wiggled down. "But Parker came over Friday night and said my action figures collection was neat."

Delta smiled as she walked Izzy to the Peugot. "We really do appreciate it that you stayed with Billy. Parker's a nice guy. He seems to be smiling a bit more lately."

"I don't know him very well. There was a storm. He came over when the lights went off." Izzy slid into the driver's seat. She backed up and around before heading down the driveway to the road. The McKenna women stood together on the lawn, waving. Izzy waved merrily back and caught just a few words of their muted conversation. As she left the Mayhill country-side, she wondered what Delta had meant by the overheard words, "Carole sure did have a good idea."

Izzy still pondered the words on Monday morning when she entered the library. She avoided the office, not wanting to miss Parker, should he decide to come to the library. He didn't.

Later, making a few wrong turns on the way home, she noticed that he wasn't sitting in front of the fire station.

She didn't see him for almost two weeks.

☙

The library didn't have much on Rosemary Mayhill, but the newspapers did. Izzy purchased a spiral notebook and wrote a year on every page, starting with 1885, the year of Rosemary's birth, and ending with 1983, her death. Each time she found mention of Rosemary, she made note of the date and recorded the event on the page corresponding with the correct year. The outdated newspapers were filled with tidbits. Izzy discovered Rosemary's favorite recipe for apple pie, and how often the woman had hosted the church's bake sales. The births of Rosemary's seven children were front-page items as was the loss of two of them to childhood diseases. When Rosemary lost a toe to frostbite, the *Mayhill Daily* was there.

After Izzy finished reading Rosemary's obituary, she sorted out the information and kept what was interesting, deciding to go to the elderly residents of Mayhill and find out more details about the events. She still needed a clearer picture of the habits and personality of Rosemary.

Over the phone Fred acted a little disappointed after finding out that Mark Dalton would not be there. Izzy did the cooking, preparing a tuna casserole to die for. Whip pitched in and whipped up a key lime pie. By the time Izzy went to fetch Fred, the kitchen aromas had her stomach growling.

A thump from Whip's fingers inspired Fred to join in the prayer. Izzy peeked during Whip's words. Fred wasn't bowing, he was staring at the food appreciatively. His fork found action before the final strain of "Amen" left Whip's mouth.

The men didn't talk while they ate. Finally, Fred sat back. "That was delicious." He took a handkerchief out of his back pocket and patted at his lips, missing a sliver of bread hanging on the edge of his lip.

Izzy sat down across from Fred and opened the notebook. "Tell me what you remember about Rosemary."

Fred grinned, slurping down a gulp of iced tea. "Old Rosemary knew how to get around the townspeople. If you didn't return a book on time, she'd come knocking at your door with her little library card list. Only two people managed to be forgiven for losing a library book. One was a migrant worker who fell in love with the words of a poet. For years Rosemary would get this dreamy expression on her face and start speculating where the book might be. She imagined it in hay wagons of Kansas, on dirt farms in Tennessee, orange groves in California. She enjoyed the musings so much that she forgave Miguel for stealing the book."

"And the other book?"

"I think I'll have another piece of that pie if you don't mind." Fred took out his handkerchief again, this time he got the piece of bread.

After three bites, Fred sat back with a contented smile and continued. "It was well after Rosemary's retirement. Oh, but she bothered Catherine Wilfong, who was the librarian who took over after Rosemary stepped down, with her suggestions and rearrangings. Nary a day went by that Rosemary didn't mosey down to the library to help out, not that Catherine wanted her to. Catherine felt quite capable of running the library herself. I suppose the second lost book really falls under Catherine's jurisdiction, but it was Rosemary who claimed credit." Fred was the only one to chuckle at the joke. "Rosemary was already well into her eighties, maybe already ninety. Her great-great-granddaughter Francine was expecting her first child. Francine was only seventeen, and everyone was worried. I was in Chicago at a conference. Those were the days." Fred nudged Whip as if they shared a secret.

"Francine wasn't due for another month, but babies being what they be, the little one decided to come early. The whole family, including Rosemary, headed for Lincoln in the dead of winter. They went to the big hospital there and in the wee hours of the morning Francine Strickland had a son, while someone stole her purse."

Izzy's head jerked up. *Strickland?* Could this possibly be Parker's mother?

"Yep, those big cities are full of crime. While Francine was cooing over Parker, an ingrate was running off with her purse. A library book was in it. Rosemary 'bout tore into Catherine when the woman started to send out an overdue notice."

"So," Izzy tried to make her voice sound steady, "Parker Strickland is Rosemary Mayhill's great-great-grandson?"

"Yep. Francine's maiden name is *Mayhill*."

Izzy's pencil broke. Fred didn't notice and continued giving insights into Rosemary's history. Izzy set the pencil aside, and Whip handed her a pen. An hour later, Fred still rambled on. He switched from detailing his own life to discussing Rosemary's to straying to other elderly residents. In the back of the spiral notebook, Izzy recorded some of the more colorful stories, thinking she'd give some suggestions to Jake about who to feature during the centennial.

It was late when Izzy returned to her apartment. Radar chomped on hard cat food. Izzy changed into her nightgown and got down on her knees beside the bed. Usually, her prayers came easily, but maybe she'd been praying the same words for so long, they were rote. The people of this small town were getting a piece of her, Izzy realized. Her prayer started with a thanks for her landlord, and a concern for Fred's health, but when she turned her prayer to concerns for Parker, she didn't know where to start.

❧

The accident happened just outside of Mayhill. Parker elevated Delta's head while wiping aside bangs and blood. Her color was good. He busily checked her vital signs. If the situation back at the car weren't so somber, Parker would have whooped when Delta opened her eyes and blinked at him once before returning to unconsciousness. Convinced that Delta wasn't in immediate danger, he glanced at the car.

"Come on!" Ty yelled, trying once again to pry the driver's-side door open. The driver slumped over the wheel.

Robert yelled, "Wait a minute! I wish backup would get here. Jeff, radio York, see what's taking them so long."

The electrical pole moved as Ty again placed one leg on the car's fender and tried to pry the door open.

"Watch it," Robert warned. The pole leaned dangerously. The momentum of a speeding car cracking into its foundation had left the man-made fixture as unstable as a rotting elm tree half sawn through at the bottom.

Precious moments ticked by while Robert readied the gas motor for the jaws of life a distance away. Officer Rowe returned from cordoning off the area. Ty helped steady the machine when Robert placed the jaws in the seams of the car's door and like a jackhammer began forcing the car door to give. Everyone breathed a sigh of relief when the jaws slid open the door, like an elevator opening, so that the young man was free.

Robert eased off just as the door creaked open. The young man flopped out. Robert caught him gently by the head, leveling him, and muttering. "I thought he was pinned." Going down to one knee, Robert felt for a pulse in the boy's neck.

"Move over." Ty joined Robert by the victim's side, immediately checking, starting CPR.

"Kyle," Ty whispered.

"The air evac will be too late," Robert said.

Parker looked from Ty to Robert. Both men were pale and shaken. They knew this boy. He'd marched in holiday parades with his lips connected to a tuba. He'd played football at Mayhill High, before going off to Lincoln on a scholarship. If only his grades had been passing, he'd have been there now, instead of lying on a dirt road with the breath knocked out of him forever and the evidence of empty beer cans, covered with blood and hair, on the floorboard. Parker and Ty went back to Delta. Right now, she was their priority.

"I don't want his name over the airwaves," Robert hissed. "I'll be the one to tell his mama, not some idiot with a squawk box who happened to catch an emergency transmission and couldn't wait to spread the news."

Ty nodded gloomily.

"And Delta's folks?" Officer Rowe joined the conversation.

"You know them better than most, Parker," Robert retrieved the paperwork from the engine. "Get on the phone. Call your mother. Have her get Delta's parents and fill them in on what's happening. What's your take on Delta?"

"She'll live. Her pulse is strong, but she's bitten through her top lip, and I'll bet her front teeth are in the car somewhere amidst the beer cans. Other than that only an X-ray will tell."

"It's four in the afternoon. On a Tuesday!" Ty said. "Why were they out drinking?"

No one answered. Robert went back to the truck. Officer Rowe stayed by Kyle, halfheartedly rechecking the boy's pulse, and then slowly covering the body with a sheet.

The sound of a tractor filled the air. Parker looked up annoyed, ready to chase the trespasser away until he realized it was the farmer who'd placed the call.

Chester Wilfong brought a gallon of cold water and a Bible. "Wife says if you be needing anything, just let her know."

Robert nodded, taking the gallon of water and turning it upright to get a swig.

The helicopter radioed its location.

Mayhill's ambulance arrived just in time to wave good-bye to the helicopter. Doctor Phil Taylor knelt beside the body. "First traffic death this year," he remarked. "Why'd it have to be someone so young?" He didn't expect an answer.

"I'll never get used to this," Parker murmured.

"And if you ever did," Robert said, "it would be time to change vocations."

Parker's shift ended at eight. He felt exhausted enough to pull his truck over to the side of the road and sleep there, but knew he needed to get home, at least to feed Brute.

At ten, the Lincoln television station covered the death of one of Mayhill's own. Pictures of Kyle flashed across the screens. Mention of his failure to succeed at the university didn't occur. The coverage of weeping parents jarred Parker.

Julia had had to be pried from a smashed vehicle. He hadn't been there to hold her head. No beer cans had rattled on the floorboard, their worthless noise claiming responsibility for one more senseless death. He'd become a fireman because of her. Because when Robert Parrish had knocked at his door, with all the compassion of a lifetime featured in his brown eyes—that had been the life thread that enabled Parker to walk out the front door and get in the back of the police car that took him to the scene of the accident, where Julia had lain stiff and cold in the back of an ambulance.

After the raw taste of pain left his throat, Parker pushed himself up and went into the kitchen to down two cold sodas in a row, ignoring the effect of acid on the raw edges of his throat. He opened a third and went into the living room, staring vaguely at the movie that followed the Tuesday night news.

&

Izzy hadn't known the young man, although she almost felt she had after listening to Carole's tears and tales. Jake Martin had come to retrieve Carole, sure that a time of mourning was necessary for his wife. After all, she'd taught Kyle in Bible school. An American flag went to half-mast outside the city hall, and the Boy Scouts immediately took out tin cans and started canvassing the neighborhoods. The parents were farmers. Money came by season and now was an uncertain time. Izzy played the closing tape to an empty library. Parents had called children home, mostly to stare at, and to appreciate the look of their offspring. Carole held her stomach as she walked out the front door. "I don't think I'll be in tomorrow," she advised. "And. . .this child will never drink anything but Kool-Aid and orange juice."

Izzy nodded. Carole was already past due and shouldn't have been working anyway. The doctor had pushed back the due date. After locking the library door and facing the sunlight, Izzy went home.

Whip had fixed meat loaf. They both sat at the kitchen table, with unmoving forks, pondering the meaning of life and feeling strangely guilty of some wrongdoing. Whip because his old age seemed ripe for death, and yet he lived on. Izzy because she had dear friends in Phoenix who sat behind the wheels of cars with the taste of liquor on their tongues and the fear of death far away. Friends who didn't understand why she preferred going to a movie rather than going to a bar. Friends who didn't understand the lure of Sunday school on a sleep-in morning. And to think, she'd thought the town of Mayhill to be so far removed from Phoenix.

The devil didn't check the map for size and population.

Izzy took a breath and stood up. The phone rang. Whip answered it. Izzy heard him grumble about good ideas and being there.

"Are they going to have a special service at church tonight?" Izzy looked at the barely touched meat loaf.

"Yes, at eight." Whip scooped the meat loaf into a covered dish and pushed it in her hands as she headed out the back door. "Parker will say he doesn't need it. Just leave it on the kitchen counter. He'll eat it."

Carefully, Izzy laid the meat loaf on her passenger side seat. Kyle wouldn't be eating meat loaf anymore. The streets were strangely silent as she drove toward Parker's. Every light in his house was on. Izzy slowed down and eased her foot off the gas, unsure if she should turn around or if she should go ahead and attempt knocking on his door. The smell of the food enabled her to push her foot to the pedal and turn in his driveway.

His curtains were open. Izzy saw his body lapped over on the couch, head hung low, hands reaching listlessly to the floor.

She knocked.

He didn't move.

She knocked again, and then she opened the door and went into the living room. "Parker," she whispered.

He raised his head. Bloodshot eyes called out to her.

"Parker, have you eaten today?"

"Who invited you in?" he muttered.

six

"Nobody invited me in. I just came." Izzy tightened her grip on the casserole dish.

"You're not wanted."

If anyone else had made that statement, Izzy would have turned and marched out the door, with a heroic slam. Instead, she clutched the meat loaf, trying to decide what to do. The look of the living room inspired her to stay more than anything. It had the look of loneliness.

"I heard about the accident." She took one step closer.

He jerked to a sitting position. His eyes penetrated hers, flashing irritation. "You don't take hints very well, do you?"

Izzy felt hot tears beginning to form. She squeezed her eyelids shut, willing the sadness to disappear, telling herself that he acted this way because he'd forgotten any other way.

He left the couch with one fluid motion. Using the shirt material bunched at her shoulders, he walked her backwards. "I want you to leave," he said slowly. "I don't need you."

His voice said one thing; his eyes another.

"Let go of me," she whispered. "You're just trying to scare me. You shouldn't be alone."

"You don't even know me." His fingers pressed into the skin of her arms. "And I don't want to know you."

He didn't mean it. Izzy wasn't sure how she knew that, but she did. Never before had she so wanted to reach out and make a difference, to fill a need, to touch a soul. This man had the ability to make her vulnerable. And she was helpless to stop him and clueless as to how to help him.

It was possible that in many ways, he was more vulnerable than she.

She whispered, "I know you need a friend."

"I need to be left alone." His hands left her shoulders.

"Hungry?" she gasped, thrusting the plate of food at him.

He backed away, shaking his head. A look of disgust, anger, loathing, and hatred filled his eyes. Not aimed at her, no, but at himself.

Izzy again offered the meat loaf. "Parker, it wasn't your fault."

"I don't want your meat loaf, and I don't want your pity." He jerked away from her, jostling her.

The meat loaf fell to the floor. Its crash resounded through the silent house and made Izzy flinch. The plastic wrap came undone. Meat lumped on his hardwood floors.

Izzy went to her knees. "Oh."

Parker hauled her back to her feet. "Leave it."

She had made things worse, again. She should have called one of the deacons. Phil Taylor would have been glad to come. For that matter, why weren't Parker's parents here? This man was too alone. Why didn't they realize what he was thinking about?

Brute howled from outside. Doggy noises distracted Izzy, but not Parker. He kept a grip on her upper arm while he ran his other hand through his hair. It stood straight up, sweat plastering it together. His jaw twitched. Right now, Izzy knew Parker was running on adrenaline and raw need. This is what happened when you didn't know the Lord. There was no one to reach out to, until you grasped at the first sign of humanity. And usually you grabbed rough.

She remembered the anger she'd felt at her father's death. How she'd wanted to hurt someone, in order to divert the pain.

"Parker, stop." Izzy pushed against him. What she really wanted to do was cradle his head between the palms of her hands and whisper that everything would be okay. That he could cry and tell her what was in his heart. "I came to tell you that they're holding a candlelight service in Kyle's memory tonight. Come with me."

He shook his head.

Tears streamed down her cheeks. Her throat constricted, and she let out a ragged breath, the sobs hitting the silence of the room. "Come on, Parker. Please."

"What are you doing, lady? You don't know me! You think it's that simple. You think I can just go to this vigil, and suddenly it will be all right."

He pushed away. Her head banged against the screen door sharply. The latch, already creaking under the pressure of holding her up, shuddered and came undone. Izzy tumbled out of the door, falling flat on her back and biting her tongue.

Parker hadn't lost his balance. He jerked the door open, staring down at her without expression. "Are you okay?"

"I think so." Izzy swallowed.

"Good. Now go home." The screen slammed shut, followed by the thud of the wooden door.

Izzy picked herself up and limped away. She should be angry. He had pushed her away, had pushed her out the door. But she wasn't angry, she was enlightened. A man who felt this much pain at the death of a child must have a sensitive heart. Once he answered God's call, this man would be a mighty Christian.

But Izzy didn't have a clue how to reach him. How to touch the vulnerable part of the man and soothe his pain. And it bothered her how much she wanted to.

Izzy didn't pray on the way to her church. She felt the presence of the Lord beside her and knew He was crying, too.

❧

Parker stared out the screen door as Brute did his business. Breaths came and went in jagged bursts. Something had to change. Every time he saw that woman, he acted irrationally. Isobelle de la Rosa: the bearer of meat loaf and talk of redemption.

"I'm sorry, Julia." He walked over to stand in front of one of the few pictures he'd left hanging. Julia's laughing eyes were caught forever in a picture-perfect moment as she flung her arms with abandonment around Parker's neck. His father had taken the photo at Mayhill Park, just two months before Julia and the car slid off the interstate and became another statistic for winter accidents.

His fist pounded against the wall, unmindful of the plaster giving way under his strength. Now, beside the picture of a couple locked in loving embrace, a portion of the wall caved in as easily as the front end of Julia's car had. Parker walked to the back door, ignoring his hand's dull pain. It was better to have an aching fist than an aching heart. Brute answered Parker's whistle, bounding up the steps and decorating Parker's pants with mud and stickers before heading to his dish, stopping in shocked dismay and trotting expectantly to sniff at the large bag of dog food.

"Okay, okay." Parker started walking into the kitchen.

Brute followed, puppy paws skidding on the floor and sending him close to the meat loaf. While Brute ate with unabashed pleasure, Parker picked up the plate. He turned the television up, hoping the noise would drown out his conscience. She had smelled so good. Her scent lingered in the living room. He hated being alone, but no way was he heading into town to sit on a hard bench pew and listen to the weeping of survivors. They'd had a candlelight vigil for Julia. Parker hadn't gone, but his parents had. They had brought an envelope full of money to the farm. The church's idea of help: prayer and money.

He'd only wanted one thing: Julia back.

He'd enjoyed being married. From the first time he'd looked at Julia and realized that he preferred to spend Saturday nights in stocking feet, watching old movies on the telly instead of prowling with the guys, to the evenings when he'd eaten her mealtime experiments—he'd been a happy guy. Content. Growing comfortable with a member of the opposite sex had become the most natural state of being to him, until his cocoon had been cruelly ripped open by a patch of ice on the interstate.

The noise from the television reached him, drawing his

attention to the screen where pictures of the afternoon's accident victim flashed. Parker picked up the remote and clicked the set off. The silence surrounded him, an accusing non-sound that created the picture of Izzy lying on his front porch where he'd allowed her to fall. For a moment he resented the fact that, lately, Isobelle de la Rosa had haunted his dreams more than Julia. Much more than Julia.

Brute came racing out of the kitchen, crumbs of meat loaf dribbling down his whiskers. He skidded sideways on the wooden floor and landed with a thump against Parker's socks.

Parker ignored him until the whining hit operatic tones. Brute jumped on the sofa and circled the cushions three times before sticking his nose against Parker's leg and falling asleep. Parker soon joined him.

☙

Carole opened the office door and peeked in. "Why are you hiding back here?"

"I'm not hiding," Izzy protested, rubbing her eyes.

"It was a late night," Carole murmured, massaging her stomach.

The candlelight service had ended at midnight. Half the town had shown up. Izzy figured the other half were still in shock. Parker hadn't shown up, although Izzy, ever hopeful, kept checking the foyer.

"That it was." Izzy rubbed her forehead.

Carole shrugged and backed out before Izzy could ask any questions. Carole was supposed to be home on bed rest until the baby came. She was going stir crazy, Izzy knew that. Okay, she'd let the "real" head librarian putter around for a while, like maybe twenty minutes. Then, Izzy would send her home. But for now, Izzy needed the down time. She wished she had been able to sleep last night. After she'd driven home, she'd eaten a grilled cheese sandwich and paced until dawn. This restlessness was alien to her. The feelings just didn't fit into her easy division of what was right and wrong. Oh, she knew the difference and how to act, but for the first time, doing right didn't come without repercussion. For the first time, she was attracted to a man who didn't have Jesus first in his life.

She had tried to think of the married couples of the Bible and found herself reaching. The heroes of the New Testament, so many were single. Finally, she settled for reading the account of Priscilla and Aquila. And when she set the Bible down, she felt somewhat renewed. A goal, her goal, was to have a mate as dedicated to the Lord as she was.

Izzy had held the Bible tight. She knew the words within. And she knew that what she was longing for wasn't for the best. Parker Strickland wasn't meant to be her mate. He might be a great rescuer of cats, a super Monopoly player, and a man who agonized over the pain of others; but he wasn't open to the teachings of the Bible. He ignored the topic every time she brought it up, which had been twice.

And, according to his journal, he was suicidal. Izzy had carefully placed her Bible on the end table. The Bible was clear about that topic. Man's body was a temple. You shouldn't mess with the temple.

Reminiscing was not getting the library open. Izzy yawned and stood up. The library opened in ten minutes; best get Carole home before regulars came in and lured the woman into conversation. Conversation that would center around Kyle.

"Does Jake know you're here?" Izzy pushed a library cart full of books behind the checkout counter.

Carole thumbed through the lost and found drawer. "He said I could come visit you for a half hour, if I promised to sit and not drink coffee."

"Okay, you've got about five minutes left." Izzy restocked the pencil holders. "I'm working on the piece about Rosemary Mayhill. Do you remember her?"

"I hear about her every night while Jake decides just how he's going to convince me to role play whatever it is you're writing about her. Apparently, he also wants there to be a conversation between a young Rosemary and an old Rosemary. I'm not sure I'm flattered about the part I get to play. The only thing I remember about her is that she gave me a chunk of peppermint candy once when I was waiting for my mama to check out some books."

"Hmmm." Izzy chewed on the pencil's eraser. "You're the fourth person to mention peppermint candy. Maybe I'll arrange for complimentary ones to be passed out while I give my presentation."

"Good idea."

"Anything else?" Izzy asked eagerly.

"Not from me."

"Think Jake would remember anything?"

"Ahem," Carole cleared her throat. "Ah, Izzy. Jake wouldn't remember much because. . .Jake is, er, seven years younger than I am."

Izzy raised her eyebrows. "Really? I never would have guessed that. I think that's wonderful. You know women out-live men by seven years, so you're a perfect match."

The advice didn't cool Carole's blush. "I tried dating other guys, but from the first time I saw him I guess I knew. He was playing baseball with my little brother, Jerry, and one of the guys hit a ball through my bedroom window. It landed right on my bed. Knocked off two of my dolls. One had a china face, and it cracked into tiny slivers of what looked like veins. Suddenly, my favorite doll looked more like a wicked witch than my treasure. Jerry came running in, asked me if I was hurt, grabbed the baseball, and left. Two of his little friends were behind him. I remember Jake asked me if I still played with dolls, and I told him no, but that one had been special.

"I guess Jerry sneaked in and got it later. Jake had asked him to. About a week later my doll sat on the bedspread with a new coat of pink paint smeared across its cheek with eight-year-old skill. I still have that doll. Whenever Jake and I have an argu-ment, I go to grandmother's whatnot cabinet and stare at that disfigured face and realize that I have the best husband in the world. You'll have that someday." Carole walked to the exit.

Izzy didn't move. Imagine knowing, having, a love like

that. Carole opened the door to leave. "By the way, I think Parker's crazy about you." Carole giggled as she left.

Izzy's pencil dropped to the floor and rolled under the desk. Opening the drawer, Izzy felt for another. There were no more. Izzy went back to the office to get a new box. Her elbow knocked against two of the many books that cluttered the desk. After a moment she gave up looking for a box of pencils, or any loose pencils on her desk for that matter. Any pencil risking refuge on her desk was buried under a mass of "things to do." Izzy scooted her chair back and dropped to her knees, stretching for the two fallen books.

She heard the door open, figured it was Carole, and called impatiently, "You're supposed to be home."

"I thought maybe I should apologize."

Parker's voice penetrated her ears. She sat up, hitting her head with a resounding thump that sent stars to her head and tears to her eyes.

"Hello, Parker." She grabbed the desk and used her hands to drag herself to a standing position. She looked at Parker. He held a baseball cap nervously in his hands and stood ramrod straight. He was the last person she wanted to see. Right?

He stopped reshaping his hat. "I wasn't myself last night. I just wanted to say I'm sorry, and it won't happen again."

"Uh, thanks, I think." Izzy bent, picked up the books from the floor, and set them back on the desk. They teetered precariously. Parker took one step and balanced them with his finger.

"Look, Parker," Izzy took a deep breath, "I didn't mean to bother you, I—"

"You didn't bother me—"

"Yes, I did. You've asked me to leave you alone and I haven't, but listen, I want to ask you something."

"What?"

"The other day, you turned in a—"

"Oh, Parker, I'm so glad you're here." Carole came unannounced through the door. "Izzy's doing some research on your great-great-grandmother. You've got some family records and photos out at the farm, don't you? Sure you do. Why don't you invite Izzy out there to look them over?"

ஃ

Parker drove away shaking his head. All he'd wanted to do was to put things right. He'd overstepped some boundaries, and it had been really rude to let Izzy lie on his porch after his door had burst open and she'd taken a tumble.

He was a paramedic! Even if his blood was boiling out of control and all the carefully constructed walls were crumbling, he should have reached out a hand and checked for injuries. Face it, the woman got under his skin. And now he'd agreed to let her stop by and go through the old family photographs.

He frowned. The apology hadn't gone quite as he'd expected. He'd wanted to humbly say his words, then slink out, but after Carole had walked in, all thoughts of setting things to right had fled. Why had he agreed to let Izzy come over? He didn't need a woman as intense, as flowery—what had Whip called Izzy?—as *good* as she was. He didn't need anyone at all, but especially not her.

Maybe he should stop fighting it, go ahead and take the girl out. See how compatible they were. No, he shook his head. Izzy was not a country girl. She might be having fun now, joining bowling leagues, sharing meals with old men, but soon she'd want a selection of malls and fancier restaurants. Besides, according to every person he knew, Izzy planned on leaving town after Carole came back from maternity leave.

The light turned red. Parker stopped the truck, glancing over downtown's Main Street. He didn't want to go home. Didn't think he could stand the silence, or the broken wall plaster by Julia's photograph, or the still-slick floor where Izzy's meat loaf had been enjoyed by Brute until only a few crumbs remained. Summers Cafe looked too busy. Parker checked out the street again. When the light changed to green, Parker pulled up next to the curb.

He'd been getting his hair cut at Matt's Barber Shop since childhood. He remembered the first time he'd followed his father into the room swirling with the heady smell of shaving cream and hair oil. He'd sat on a black folding chair and read a comic while Matt snipped at what was left of Grant Strickland's hair. Dad had admired the cut, made a quick rearrangement to the top, and then turned to plop Parker into the brown vinyl barber's chair where three Lincoln phone books waited. Matt had draped a dark cape under Parker's chin and begun cutting the brown curls that his mother adored and Rhea envied. To Parker, sitting in the barber shop had been the first step into manhood. He'd listened to the snip of the barber's shears while staring at his wrinkled boots and noticing they were smaller versions of his father's. He'd left the barber shop that first time feeling taller.

"Hi, Parker, thought you'd started cutting your hair yourself." Matt trimmed the white sides on Whip's head. Parker sat down without answering and idly thumbed an ancient comic, wondering if it was left over from his childhood.

Whip stared with bright chuckles in his eyes. Parker looked away, wondering if Izzy had told Whip that he'd thrown the meat loaf on the floor during a fit of passion.

Matt looked out the window. "Winter's coming."

"Yep," Parker agreed.

"I hear Izzy's writing a story about Rosemary. You're having her over tomorrow night? Are you taking her to your folks' house, or to your place?" Whip grinned foolishly, as if the idea had been his.

"That Izzy, she's a looker." Matt held the scissors in the air and studied Whip's gray locks with a short black comb suspended in the air.

"My place, but it's nothing to get excited about. I'll show her some old pictures, she'll write a cute story, and that's it." Parker felt the pressure building. He'd just left the library, and already people knew Izzy was coming over to his house tomorrow night.

❧

The house was dark when Izzy pulled into the driveway.

Grabbing a soda, she headed upstairs. She turned the television on and sat cross-legged on the floor in front of the coffee table and opened her spiral notebook.

She'd accomplished quite a lot the last few days. Over half the notebook pages had at least something scribbled on them. She began rewording her research. In red, she highlighted some potential questions for Parker, knowing he wouldn't be able to answer them, but maybe he'd take her with him over to his family's house to ask them.

What she wanted the most was to make sure that she had enough questions to keep him occupied and his mind off. . . well, off her.

Izzy sat back. Why did she want Parker to take her to his parents' house? She knew Mr. and Mrs. Strickland. She bowled with them. Radar crawled into her lap. She didn't bother to push the cat away as she usually did when she was working. She wanted Parker to take her to his parents' house because she wanted them to get used to her. Because no matter how much she denied it, she was falling in love with Parker.

In love with Parker?

In love?

Izzy laid her head on the coffee table. Love with a man who often told her to leave him alone? No, he didn't just *tell* her to leave him alone, he *ordered* her to leave him alone. And allowed her to fall to the ground without offering a hand to help her up! And treated her without respect! And didn't go to church!

"Oh, Radar," she moaned, scooping the cat into a hug. "What am I going to do?"

The cat wiggled free, not in the mood to be pampered. Izzy watched the tail go straight up in the air as Radar went to look disdainfully at the store-bought cat food that had replaced the liver Whip had been feeding him. Izzy rolled her eyes. Lately no one seemed to appreciate the food she gave them. Thinking about food reminded her that she hadn't really gotten much nourishment from the frozen dinner. She pushed herself up off the floor and headed downstairs.

seven

Parker drove down the street, glancing in the mirror occasionally to admire his haircut. It looked good, better than when his mother trimmed it. He shook his head; things were changing, whether he wanted them to or not.

Turning off Main Street, Parker pulled his car in front of the familiar structure that had been his home for the first eighteen years of his life. It was a yellow clapboard monstrosity, added on to by expanding branches of the Strickland family. He parked the truck in the street, dismayed at the sight of Aunt Edna's car in the driveway. He sat a moment, contemplating, then he got out of the car and headed up the sidewalk.

His foot rested on the first porch step and he paused, once again considering turning around. Aunt Edna's voice carried from the living room, blasting through the open screen door. Parker winced.

"This is ridiculous! How dare they claim Kenny to be undesirable for service! They only gave him three weeks!"

"Now, Edna," Grant Strickland soothed, "you said yourself you didn't want Kenny going overseas. At least now you know there's no chance of that."

Parker left his hand on the doorknob, listening to his father, and steeling himself for the family argument he was about to join. He stepped inside. No one in the living room turned to acknowledge him.

Edna stood in the middle of the room. Her fists were clenched. "Do you think that comforts me?" Her cheeks went red with rage as she noticed Parker with a glare. "The paper will print lies, and everyone will think my boy's unfit!"

Slouched in the green easy chair, Kenny balanced a beer bottle on his knee and dangled a cigarette from his lips. His

89

eyes already red and wild. The reddish-brown hair that so resembled Parker's stood at attention, the only part of his body still looking military.

Edna moved to stand in front of the television, an unyielding granite of indignation. Her hand shook as she waved a piece of paper in Parker's direction with short, threatening jerks. "We're going to fight this!"

The phone rang, startling Parker's mother and saving Parker from having to answer. Francine grabbed at the receiver, knocking it to the ground with a clang. She nervously settled it to her ear. "Hello."

Parker watched her eyebrows rise as she listened intently to the person on the other end, occasionally opening her mouth to offer a response, but never getting the chance. After a few minutes, without saying good-bye, Francine numbly put the receiver back to the phone and whispered, "That was Blanche McKenna."

Edna eased up, shaking the paper at Parker, and glanced uneasily between Francine and Kenny. "What did she want?"

"They're coming over." Francine pushed herself up off the couch and began picking up the newspaper that Grant had dropped on the floor.

"Did she say why?" Grant asked.

"Delta's not doing too well. They need to go to Lincoln for a few weeks to be with her."

"What's that got to do with us?" Grant quizzed.

"Not us," Francine said softly. She shot a worried glance at Kenny, looking disapprovingly at the cigarette.

Kenny set his beer on the end table, carefully twirling the bottle so that it rested on the round ring of condensation already there, and stubbed out the butt on a plate. "What's wrong with Delta?" he slurred.

"She was in an automobile accident." Parker spoke for the first time.

"That has nothing to do with us!" Edna snapped. "Kenny wasn't even back in town!" She walked over and snatched the beer bottle from his grasp.

"Shut up, Mother." Kenny stood, ambled to the kitchen and returned with a cold one.

Edna's mouth closed. The paper in her hand dropped to the floor. Francine took her sister by the shoulders and led her into the kitchen. Grant followed.

Parker picked up the official-looking piece of paper and glanced over it quickly.

"I didn't do nothing," Kenny defended himself after Parker placed the dishonorable discharge notice on the television.

"Of course not." Parker rolled his eyes.

"She flirted with me and when I acted on it, she complained. Said I wouldn't leave her alone. Why else would a woman join the service, if not to find a man?"

Parker didn't answer. He'd rather have a woman defending the nation than Kenny, but this was not the time to tell Kenny that.

"Why do you think the McKennas are coming over?" Parker changed the subject.

"How should I know?"

"It must have something to do with you."

"I hardly ever see Delta. She hasn't talked to me since she had the kid. Over five years. I didn't even know she was in the hospital."

"Don't you want to know how she is?"

Kenny raised red-rimmed eyes. "Sure, tell me."

"Her concussion is mild. That's not worrying the doctors, but she wrenched her back upon collision. They're diagnosing acute lumbar strain. She'll go through months of therapy trying to restore easy movement. Her front teeth are missing. I guess Mr. McKenna went to the yard and dug through the car hoping to locate them, but no luck—"

"When was the last time you had anything to do with Delta?" Grant came back into the room and sat on the arm of the couch, interrupting their conversation and glaring at Kenny.

"High school," Kenny mumbled, lowering his eyes.

"She hasn't written, contacted you, anything, since?"

"No, she and her parents avoid me like the plague."

"Well, it looks like—"

The squeal of tires and slamming doors silenced Grant.

Thomas McKenna didn't knock. He jerked open the screen door and strode into the room. His usually serious eyes focused on Kenny in a heated stare. He ignored Parker and Grant. Blanche was only a step behind, holding Billy's hand.

"We're leaving for Lincoln tonight," Thomas ground out.

"Thomas, Billy can come with us—" Blanche said.

"Delta needs us. She's alone in that hospital up there, and driving back and forth is wiping you out." Thomas glared at Kenny, before touching his wife's shoulder.

Kenny didn't look up.

"We warned Delta about you," Thomas continued. "She wouldn't listen. Said that underneath it all you were a real nice guy—"

Edna and Francine came to the kitchen door, staring into the living room with worry. Blanche picked up Billy. She stepped toward Edna and Francine, but looked at her husband. "I'm not sure about this, Thomas."

Without a word, Edna and Francine moved aside to let Blanche pass. Billy stared back at the living room as if knowing that it was his future they were going to play ping-pong with. Giving Kenny one last openmouthed stare, Edna hurried into the kitchen. For the first time, Parker thought about Billy's age and how Kenny had hung around Delta in high school. No, that couldn't be it. If Billy belonged to any of Parker's relatives, he belonged to Chris. Delta had only hung around Kenny for a short time. *Of course,* Parker realized, watching Kenny's ears turn red, *a short time is all that is needed.*

Thomas stood in the middle of the room, looking ridiculously like Edna a few minutes ago. The man seemed ready to explode. "Mr. McKenna," Parker said gently. "Maybe if you'll just tell us what's going on, we can help."

"Can't you guess, Parker?" Grant went to the middle of the room and touched Thomas' arm, motioning him to the couch. "Billy is Kenny's son, isn't he?"

Thomas nodded, all the anger vanishing, as if no energy remained.

"Why are you coming to us now?" Grant sat down next to Thomas. Parker watched as Kenny closed his eyes.

"Oh, I know the Strickland family would have wanted to do right by my girl, but I don't consider Kenny part of your family," Thomas continued.

Kenny didn't move, but his bloodshot eyes opened and glared at Thomas.

"I would rather claim Delta didn't know the father than have the town know Kenny was the one," Thomas said.

Kenny reached, without looking, for the bottle of beer and took a drink.

"We stood by her." Thomas looked as if he was trying to convince himself. "She wanted to keep the baby. We went along with it. Mother thought things would be all right. Delta took over the books, got her GED, and actually was doing a pretty good job of raising Billy. We thought things were going just fine."

He no longer spoke to the family. Thomas spoke to the ceiling, his eyes taking in every detail, as if he were embarrassed. "We didn't raise her to be wild. Her older sisters were never that way. Billy did a lot to calm her down. We thought someday—prayed that someday—she'd meet the right man, settle down, and all her drinking and partying would stop.

"We never intended to let anyone know that Billy belonged to Kenny." Thomas gave Kenny another scorching look. "She didn't drink until she started up with you. Now she's in the hospital."

"She's going to be—" Parker started to say.

"I know that." Thomas tried to pull himself together. "But don't you see? Her behavior tells us that we expected too much of her. It's time for Kenny to pitch in and help. If people talk, so be it. Delta needs our attention now."

Grant stood, went into the kitchen, and came back with a cup of coffee. He handed it to Mr. McKenna. "And what do you want from us?"

"It's time for Kenny to take responsibility for his actions, at least monetarily. Delta's not going to be able to work for quite a while. Kenny must start paying her some sort of child support."

"He'll pay the child support," Edna said from the kitchen doorway.

Kenny finally moved, "Mom, we're not sure. . ."

"Oh, yes we are. You think I wouldn't recognize my own blood? I've noticed the resemblance, but I thought Chris. . . To think I've been a grandmother for five years. I put too much stock in the gossip of others. All this time I've been harboring a grudge against Chris for not living up to his raising, and it was my own boy. Blanche and I have made some decisions. When Delta's out of the hospital, we'll sit down and firm up what needs to be done. In the meantime, just tell us what you need."

❧

Izzy pulled the car into Parker's driveway. The farm looked deserted. Surely he hadn't forgotten that he'd agreed to meet with her and let her go through his family photographs. Brute's high-pitched barks sounded from around back. Izzy got out of the car and followed the noise to survey the vacant backyard and empty garage. She'd just driven all this way for nothing. Parker wasn't home.

The distant chirping of birds convinced her that the trip hadn't been completely worthless. Parker's farm had enough scenery to keep her occupied until his return. Izzy laid her purse on the back step and sat down to wait. Surely Parker would be home soon. Stretching her legs out in front of her, she surveyed his land and bounced her keys against her knees liking the way the clang contrasted with the music of nature.

Parker's place went on for miles. Trees formed one continual backdrop for the sky. The scent of dirt and foliage erased the tension at the base of her neck. The country had a lot to offer. She slipped off her sweater and leaned back. Taking a deep breath, she tried to picture what it would be like living here. This was God's country. If she lived on Parker's farm, she would never turn on the television. She would put a quilting frame on the front porch and glory in the sunsets.

After almost an hour, Izzy was tired of waiting. She grabbed her purse and headed back to the car. It was only six o'clock. Daylight was fading fast. She had never driven farther than Parker's house; maybe now would be a good time for exploring. Instead of heading home, she turned the opposite way and bumped along the uneven dirt road. A few times she passed the remains of a long-deserted building. If it had been the middle of the day, she'd have climbed out of the car and investigated. Maybe Rosemary's migrant worker had stayed here. According to Izzy's father, search far enough back in the de la Rosa history, and there were plenty of laborers.

The first hint of twilight made her decide to turn around. A driveway beckoned her, she whipped in, intending to turn around, but the porch light went on. Izzy didn't even know who lived here. A stooped, gray-haired woman in a flowered housedress stepped out on the porch. Izzy let out her breath. It was Catherine Wilfong, the woman who'd been the librarian after Rosemary. Before Carole.

"Hi, Catherine," Izzy called getting out of the car. Maybe she could ask Catherine some of the questions she had about Rosemary.

"Izzy. I've been wishing we could talk. How's the library? I keep telling my husband that I want to get to town. Come in. We were about to have supper. Glad to have the company."

If her stomach hadn't growled at that moment, Izzy might have begged off. Catherine's cooking was famous throughout Mayhill. A self-published cookbook occupied a special shelf at the library: Catherine's recipes, written down for the next generation. It was checked out often.

"Is Parker home already?" Catherine moved away from the door and welcomed Izzy in.

"No." Izzy didn't even pretend that she hadn't just been at his house. "I waited for nearly an hour. When he didn't come home, I decided to explore the area."

"Gladys Hepfield called when she saw you driving out of the city limit. She was surprised you didn't know Parker wouldn't be home."

"Where is Parker?"

"He's at his parents' house, and Delta's parents are there, too."

Izzy felt remorseful for a moment. She needed to call Delta's parents to let them know she was praying for Delta. She followed Catherine into the kitchen. "Why are Delta's parents over at the Stricklands'?"

"I don't know the whole story." Catherine said the words, but her eyes lit up. "Gladys says that the truth about Delta's son is about to be found out. Apparently, it's time for the father to pitch in. Funny, I always assumed it was Chris."

Izzy blinked, but tried not to let her emotions show. "Why are they at Parker's house?"

"Why, I suppose Parker is the father." Catherine began setting hot dishes on the table. "What's wrong?"

Izzy pictured Parker: sitting in his house agonized because he hadn't been able to save Kyle; missing his wife so much that he contemplated ending his own life; playing Monopoly all night to keep a neighbor from being scared. That type of man wouldn't, couldn't, turn his back on his own child. "Catherine, I don't think Parker is the father." No, not Parker Strickland. Izzy remembered the way he had sat on a tiny chair in the children's section of the library, surrounded by small children, pretending to be interested in the exploits of an orange dinosaur. She remembered how he had climbed the tree to get her cat. No, Parker Strickland was not Billy's father, because if he was—Billy's paternal heritage would never have been a secret.

"Evening, Izzy." Catherine's husband walked through the back door and smiled. "You waiting for Parker? He'll likely be a while."

Catherine nodded. "We enjoy company. Don't get much out here."

Izzy smiled and picked up a dish of mashed potatoes. She wasn't quite sure how she came to have such a strong conviction concerning Parker's innocence, but the sincere belief set well in her heart.

❧

Parker groaned when he saw Izzy's sweater on his porch. He'd completely forgotten that he'd invited her over. He picked the sweater up and let himself in through the door.

"Izzy," he called. Though why he bothered was a mystery. Her car wasn't outside. Silence greeted him. Obviously she hadn't entered the house. Probably she hadn't gotten over the big-city belief in locked doors. He put her sweater on the counter and opened the refrigerator. Two peanut butter and jelly sandwiches later he felt better. He picked up the phone and dialed her number. She'd be relieved to know she hadn't lost her sweater. Except, no one answered.

He thought back on the evening's events as he listened to the continual ringing. The McKennas had stayed quite a while, talking over how to ease Billy into knowing his true father. Thomas admitted that he'd never intended on just dropping Billy in Kenny's lap. All along he'd wanted Edna and the Stricklands to be the ones to pitch in and help. The rest of the family, except for Kenny, had still been making plans when Parker had left.

A scratching on the back door reminded Parker that Brute needed in. He hung up the phone, stretched, and ambled to the kitchen, opening the screen.

"Down." He laughed as the puppy jumped against his knee. After a few moments of play, Brute settled down allowing Parker to reach for the phone again.

"Hi, it's me," he said when Izzy answered. "You left your sweater."

❧

Izzy hung up the phone. Parker had called her. For the first time, he had reached out to her. She was surprised at how good that made her feel, how special. Never mind that the main topic had been her sweater.

The house was silent. Izzy turned out all the lights and sat down with Radar in her lap. The cat burrowed his nose into the crook of her arm and snoozed happily. Izzy leaned back, not wanting the television or the radio to disturb her meditating. After a few moments of staring at the ceiling, she put the cat on the couch and went in the bedroom to pull out the box of old photograph albums from under her bed. She loved looking at the pictures of her mother and father on their wedding day. Clara's red hair had been almost to her knees. Izzy's father, Rueben de la Rosa, looked like a movie star in his rented tux. They had been so happy. Rueben had wanted lots of children, but they had only been blessed—their words not hers—with one. She had been her father's little girl. Oh, and he had been strict. She had to wear dresses to church when the other girls wore jeans. She had been the last allowed to wear eye shadow. The boys she dated had to come to the door. Touching a finger to the likeness of her father, she remembered the sound of his voice, the lingering scent of his aftershave, the way he had always touched her on her shoulder as if to remind her that he was there.

He would have liked Parker Strickland.

❧

"You got your ears lowered." Ty Horner teased as Parker entered the fire station.

Absently, Parker ran his hand through the shorn locks. With everything that had happened, he had forgotten. His parents hadn't even noticed.

"It was getting a little long." Parker shrugged.

As Robert slammed his locker shut, he surveyed Parker.

"Out to impress anyone? Wife said she saw Izzy de la Rosa heading down the road your way."

"She was coming to see me, but I was at my mother's."

Ty and Robert nodded, the smiles leaving their faces, and said in unison, "We heard."

Robert put a hand on Parker's shoulder. "What's Kenny going to do?"

"Mom called this morning. Edna came over and got them out of bed about six. He just took off."

"That's better than having him live with you," Ty said.

"Yeah, but Thomas is bringing Billy over to Edna's today. She's going to start baby-sitting."

Robert frowned. "Edna's well past sixty."

"I know, and she had a hard time when Kenny was a baby."

"I remember," Robert said. "What a surprise. The doctor told Edna she couldn't have children, and then when she was forty-two, along came Kenny."

"She spoiled him," Parker said to Ty, as if the other man didn't know.

"She's more excitable now than she was then. Having a child in the house will just about send her over the edge," Robert went on.

"Will your folks help Billy, then?"

"I don't know," Parker said. "I just don't know."

Robert nodded in sympathy. "If you need time off, we can arrange it."

"I need to work."

≈

"The baby's dropped." Carole rubbed her stomach. Her face glowed with happiness. "They said I should get packed and ready. Can you believe they want me to go to Lincoln just because I'm over forty? I feel great!"

Shaking her finger at Carole, Izzy said, "I just found *Moby Dick* in the pet-care section. I had forgotten the joys of having a student assistant."

Carole laughed. "I'll bet Shannon was concerned because

there were no books on how to care for your pet whale."

"Funny," Izzy tried to look stern.

"So," Carole said nonchalantly, "what's going on with you and Parker?"

This time, Izzy's stern look was real.

The edge of Carole's mouth raised. "Okay, I give in. I won't pester you any more for information you don't want to share. But if I find out you told someone else first, I'm going to bean you with this *Moby Dick* book."

Giggling, Carole started to leave. She gave a little jump when she got to the door and patted her stomach. "Oh, he kicked, hard. He's ready; now if he'd only do something about it."

Carole stopped with that. Izzy had the funniest feeling that Carole had been imputing the same characteristics to Parker as she had to the baby. Carole's knowing grin changed the funny feeling to a convinced feeling.

"Bye," sang Carole.

"That woman's too happy," Izzy mumbled as she started entering the overdue notices. That finished, she began replacing the due date peels in the back of popular paperbacks. Country music played in the background. Izzy had fought for the music. Jake Martin claimed he'd never heard of a library with music. He said libraries were places where the word *Shhh* should be revered.

Izzy made sure the music was so low that it wouldn't disturb patrons. It really could only be heard when everyone was quiet. During peak library hours, no one noticed it. Jake Martin himself had strolled in one busy Saturday afternoon and remarked that he appreciated Izzy not using the radio. Izzy wisely kept her mouth shut and didn't tell him that the only reason he couldn't hear it was that he was not honoring the *Shhh* tradition.

eight

It was past time to get back to work. Izzy had spent too much time staring out the window, looking for Parker to bring her sweater. Actually, she cared little about the sweater; she cared more that Parker was coming. Circling the desk, Izzy settled back in her chair and picked up her book order forms. Saturdays were supposed to be busier. At least busy enough to keep her mind off an appealing fireman.

She'd finish updating the new releases. The phone rang as she chewed on her pen. Izzy waited a moment before answering it, wanting to compose herself just in case it was Parker. "Hello."

"Izzy," Mayor Martin's voice boomed, "how's our story going? Mark says he's making progress. I thought maybe we'd meet for breakfast on Monday and go over the presentations. Carole told me your idea about handing out peppermints. I think that's perfect. Can you meet at eight?"

"Jake, with Carole on maternity leave, my time is precious."

"By the way," Jake gushed on, "are you ready for three new computers?"

"I'll be there," Izzy promised, "but can we make it ten o'clock? I have other things to do on Monday morning. The story's coming along just fine." Opening a desk drawer, Izzy took out a spiral notebook. She braced it against a stack of books to the side of her computer and started typing in all the information she'd gathered. She eliminated the outline form and wrote it as if she were telling a story to a friend. She frowned after she'd written five pages. The facts were all there, but the substance was missing. She couldn't catch the essence of Rosemary Mayhill if she didn't talk to the family, look at the photographs, and dig deeper for the emotional side of Rosemary, not just rehash the time line of good deeds documented in the newspaper.

Maybe it was time to arrange a visit with Francine Strickland. Parker's mother probably had more memorabilia than Parker. Plus, getting to know Francine would give Izzy more insight into Parker's personality. The man she was dreaming about—was falling in love with—certainly didn't appear the type to be suicidal. So, what should Izzy do about the journal's desperate message? Could Parker have written it when he was in high school? Izzy sighed. The more she got to know Parker, the more confused she became. Nothing made sense.

She had set out to save Parker Strickland's life, now she worried more about his soul. She grabbed the telephone and jabbed at the numbers. No one answered the Strickland phone. Izzy glanced over at the clock. Two hours until the library closed.

The time dragged. Izzy managed to clear a corner of the desk and finish writing the grant proposal for the funding of a new multicultural section for the library. She hadn't left the office once. Shannon poked her head through the door a few times, asking senseless questions. Izzy almost suspected that the student aide was worried about her.

"Ahem."

This time when Shannon interrupted, Izzy looked up disgruntled.

"Six o'clock." Shannon pointed to her watch. Getting off on time on a Saturday was important to the girl.

"Has everyone left?"

"Twenty minutes ago."

"You go ahead and take off. It will only take me a minute to close up." Izzy stuffed the spiral notebook into her bag and stood up. If she hurried, it would still be daylight when she knocked on the Stricklands' door.

❧

Parker recognized the car. He had meant to take her sweater over, but time had gotten out of hand.

"Why's Miss Izzy here?" Billy came and yanked the curtain aside to stare out.

"We'll soon find out." Parker watched Izzy pat her hair into place. She glanced up when Billy opened the drapes.

Parker opened the door before she could knock. "You do get around, Ms. de la Rose."

"It's *de la Rosa*. I was hoping to talk with your mother. I wanted to see if she had any pictures or memories of Rosemary she'd like to share."

"Mom left for Lincoln. Dad's out shopping for Billy. Seems to think it's pretty exciting, finding he has a grandnephew."

"I want to go see Mom," Billy said, a frown creasing his brow.

Parker looked down as if he'd forgotten the boy standing there. "I know you do, Buster. Delta says she'd rather you not miss any school."

"Not fair," Billy muttered. "She's my mother and nobody tells me anything."

"Your mother feels well enough to say that you can't miss school," Izzy said. "Sounds like she's doing fine."

Billy went to the couch and sat down, arms crossed and lips pouting. Brute jumped up next to the boy.

"Come in," Parker said pretending to be gruff. He wanted to feel nonchalant—uninterested—instead he was pleased that she'd come to the house. "I'll run up to the attic and get the hope chest that has Rosemary's things in it."

He took the stairs two at a time. He knew right where the small chest was. Picking it up, he carefully made his way to the hallway. He watched Izzy as she tried to soothe Billy.

"It's not easy when Mom's sick, is it?" Izzy played with the strap of her purse.

Billy rolled his eyes.

"Oh, you think I don't know," Izzy tried to sound hurt. "I'm in Mayhill because my mother got sick. She's all better now. As a matter of fact, she feels so good that she went to Florida on a long vacation. As soon as she's well, I can go back to Phoenix."

"Why would you want to go there?"

"That's where my job is. My friends. It's where I made my home."

"You work at the library. You're friends with Parker. If your mom is here, how can your home be somewhere else?"

"That's only temporary."

Billy frowned, clearly not understanding. "What's temprary? What do you mean?"

"Carole can run the library when I leave. Parker and I have a different outlook on life, but you're right, he is my friend. Mom has Harve, but I always come to see her for the holidays."

"Where's Phoenix? Is it next to Lincoln? That's not too far away. Parker can still see you."

"Phoenix is a lot farther than that, Billy." Parker set the hope chest carefully on the floor. He eyed Izzy with disapproval. "Izzy thinks big cities are better than small towns. Don't you, Izzy?

"Ah, spiderwebs." Billy looked at the chest with interest, saving Izzy from having to answer.

"They'll take just a moment to clean away." Parker went to the kitchen and came back with a handful of paper towels. "No one's been through this thing in years. Rhea used to get the clothes out and prance around in them. I'll bet she's forgotten."

"It's beautiful." Izzy admired the intricate designs. An engraved array of flowers decorated the front; the scars and knicks of time added jagged flaws to the wood.

Parker gave the chest a second look, clearly unaware of the magic. "It should be tossed."

"Oh, no, Parker. It's a treasure. Just think of what it would look like after being refinished."

Billy got down on his knees beside Izzy. Together they unlatched the lock and raised the lid. A fine spray of dust rose in the air. Watching Izzy dig through his family treasures brought back memories. Her words about refinishing sounded too much like Julia. Only Izzy was smarter than Julia. Izzy would be going back to Phoenix soon. Back to the malls and traffic jams. Away from snow. Away from him.

"That's Grandma—when she was young! She has some pictures like this on the living room walls!" Billy shouted delightedly, coming across a picture of Rosemary with Blanche.

Parker went into the kitchen and poured a cup of coffee. Sitting at the kitchen table, Parker stared past his mother's crinoline curtains and watched the stars. The scene in the living room hurt too much.

"Parker?" Izzy said from the door.

"Yeah?" Parker looked up.

"It's getting late. I'd like to come over again to talk with you when you're not so busy. Can I take these two journals home?"

"Sure, go ahead."

"Thanks. Oh, and Parker."

"What." Impatience tinged his voice.

"Why don't you come to church with me Sunday morning?"

He stared at his coffee cup. Crazy woman, still thought that all the answers could be found in prayer. "I'm sorry, Izzy. I'm not interested."

Izzy waited, seeming to want him to say something, do something. When he made no move, she backed away. She looked down at the ground. "We keep saying 'sorry.' "

"It's best that way. You'll be leaving soon, remember?"

Her face fell, and all the sparkle left her eyes in a blink. She seemed to want to say something. Parker waited, giving her time, but she turned and went back into the living room.

He heard her softly saying good-bye to Billy as she gathered her belongings and left. Billy came into the kitchen, carrying the old photo of Rosemary and Blanche.

"Can I haf this picture?"

Parker almost retorted that Billy couldn't haf the picture, but must take it all. "Sure, Billy. Keep it."

"Grandma looks like Mama."

Parker took the picture. "She sure does. You look like her, too."

"Good," Billy said a little strongly. "I don't want to look like Kenny."

"Kenny's got some problems, Billy. Someday he'll straighten up, and you'll be proud he's your papa." Parker didn't believe the words even as they exited his mouth. He wanted to, though. He remembered when young Kenny used to tag along. They had fished, played tag, climbed the old tree at the library.

"Grandpa says it's Kenny's fault that Mama was in the accident. Grandpa said it was Kenny started Mama to drinking."

Parker didn't know how to respond. Just what was keeping Dad, anyway?

"It's getting late." Parker stood, taking Billy by the hand, hoping that being tucked into bed would calm Billy's trembling lower lip.

"I don't want to go to bed. I want my mother."

"Your mother's in Lincoln." Parker guided Billy toward the stairs. "She's in the hospital being taken care of by doctors. Doctors who will make sure she's all right."

"She needs me."

Parker opened the guest room door. "You're right. She needs you to be a good boy and go to school."

"There's no school tomorrow. It's Sunday."

Parker felt lost. Billy was right. There was no school tomorrow, and Parker was off. He'd have the care of the boy all day. The boy who was asking questions.

Billy reluctantly got into his pajamas and crawled in the strange bed. He frowned at Parker, as if it were Parker's fault that everything was going wrong.

"Night, Buster." Parker tried to sound reassuring.

"I want my mother," Billy whimpered one more time.

Parker silently made his way downstairs, relieved to hear the front door open. "Where have you been, Dad?"

"You wouldn't believe it. I knew a growing boy needed lot of milk and vegetables, so I went to the store. I couldn't make it through an aisle without someone stopping me to ask me what was going on with Kenny."

Parker watched his father. Grant never was a good liar.

"Dad."

"Okay," Grant sighed. "I ran into Carole Martin at the grocery store. She told me Izzy was visiting you and suggested I give you a little privacy."

"Privacy? Dad, Billy was here."

"Wasn't that child in bed at eight?"

"Ah." Parker hadn't even considered what a six-year-old's bedtime should be.

Grant shook his head, handed Parker the bag of groceries, and headed up the stairs.

Parker carried the food into the kitchen and set the bag on the counter. He'd just put the milk away when he heard his father holler down, "Parker! Where'd you put Billy?"

"He's in Rhea's old room!"

"No. He's not."

Parker flew up the stairs, Billy's last words playing through his head. Parker had no doubt. Billy had crawled out the bedroom window and taken off to find his mother.

❧

Izzy stuck the cup of hot chocolate in the microwave. Parker had turned down her invitation to church. That didn't mean she would give up. Statistics claimed that most new Christians came to the faith because a friend reached out to them. She would keep reaching. Parker was a smart man. He could only resist the truth for so long. Right? Izzy wished she knew the answer.

The microwave beeped. Izzy took the hot chocolate out and blew at the steam. Whip had prepared some food, too. She covered the spaghetti and put it in the refrigerator. Carefully, she carried the cocoa up to her apartment. Radar waited impatiently at the top of the stairs, meowing scoldings at a mistress too long gone. Izzy set the cocoa on the coffee table and took Radar in her lap.

"It's okay, boy. I'm home now. Where do you want to be

scratched? Behind the ears?"

After a few minutes of fur rearranging, Izzy settled back and chose the older-looking diary. Opening it to the first page, she began reading. It didn't take long to become absorbed. Rosemary had strayed from the usual day-to-day listing of events, instead she had penned a first-person narrative. Izzy grinned, Rosemary had no doubt been a fan of Louisa May Alcott.

It was midnight when the blinking lights went down the street, sending a red and white glare into Izzy's living room and making her put down the diary. She got up and went to the window. One of Mayhill's police cruisers slowly drove down the street. Izzy shivered. That was another thing she didn't miss about Phoenix, the sound of a helicopter circling overhead whenever a major crime had been committed. Izzy wondered what the policeman was looking for, or whom?

She put her shoes back on and silently went down the stairs. She'd just reached the last step when the phone rang, its shrill sound making her jump. Whip's phone never rang after midnight. Concern prickled up her spine.

Whip stumbled into the living room. Izzy couldn't see him, but she could hear him. He'd probably slipped into his robe and slippers, just in case Izzy walked in on him.

"What?" he rasped into the phone.

Izzy leaned forward. She could barely hear.

"No kidding," Whip's voice rose. "They've called out the volunteers? How long has he been missing? No, no, I'm glad you called. I'll put my pants on and start checking all the backyards in my neighborhood. Sure, I'll wake her up, but I don't think she knows anything. The fact that she's interested in Parker has nothing to do with Billy running away."

Izzy stood. Interested in Parker? Billy had run away! She rushed into the living room.

"Ask them how long Billy's been missing?"

"They discovered the boy missing at about 9:30 P.M."

"I left there at nine o'clock," Izzy said. "Billy was upset about his mother, but we thought he'd gotten over it. He wanted to go see her." Her eyes widened. "You don't think the child's heading for Lincoln, do you?"

Whip said a few more words into the phone and then hung up. "That's what Parker thinks. The state troopers have been informed. Still, there's a good chance the little boy will stop to rest before he even makes it out of town. That's what we're hoping for. I'm going to check the neighborhood."

Izzy watched Whip hurry into his bedroom to change. Calmly she picked up the phone, paused to say a prayer, and dialed Parker's number.

Francine answered.

Izzy cleared her throat. "Hello, Francine. This is Izzy de la Rosa. I just found out about Billy. Is there anything I can do?"

"Officer Rowe's on his way over to your apartment now." Francine sounded out of breath. "He wants you to try to think of anything Billy said tonight while you were over. Maybe he—" Francine choked off, weeping loudly into the phone. "Oh, what am I going to tell Delta? When I left her tonight. . ."

"Izzy," Carole's voice came over the wire. "Francine isn't able to talk. You answer all the police officer's questions and then call us back."

Personally, Izzy agreed with Parker. Billy was attempting to find his way to Lincoln so he could see his mother. She liked the police officer's idea too, that Billy would get tired and stop to rest.

The police cruiser stopped in front of the house. Whip opened the door and invited Officer Rowe and Grant Strickland in. The interview took only ten minutes.

"Yep," said Officer Rowe, "everything you said matches what Parker remembered. Don't worry. We'll find the boy."

Whip handed the men mugs of cocoa and walked the officer to his car. Izzy stayed on Whip's couch a moment. She knew she should call Francine, fill the woman in on what the officer had said, but she wanted to do more.

She wanted to find Billy.

And she had an idea.

nine

Whip wasn't the only one out searching for Billy. Flashlights galore bobbed up and down the Mayhill streets. A chorus of "Billy!" rang out in disjointed ranges of octaves. Izzy pulled her sweater closer.

Izzy paused, watching Whip. She looked up to the starry sky and closed her eyes. *O Lord, please watch over our Billy. He's so young and afraid. Keep him safe, Lord. Help us to find him soon. And, please Lord, be with his family. They have so much to worry about right now. Let them feel Your protection and love. Help me to feel it, too.* She almost uttered "Amen," but a nagging thought stopped her. She was forgetting something, someone. *And Lord, please be with Parker. Help him to recognize Your ways and to lean towards Your guidance and love. Amen.*

Whip rambled over to the hedge that separated his yard from the one next door. His raspy voice crooned "Billy" as if he were looking to wake a child from slumber.

Izzy didn't for a moment think that Billy was asleep. She'd run away from home once, when she was young. At Christmastime, no less. She hadn't thought to wear a coat that long ago day either as she ran through the darkened streets to her friend Melanie's house. Once she'd gotten there, she'd been too afraid to rap on Melanie's window. So she'd turned around, hurried toward home, and crawled back through her bedroom window. No one ever found out about her late-night escapade. Being outdoors past your bedtime wasn't conducive to sleep. Izzy couldn't remember what traumatic happening had inspired her to climb out of her window, but she did remember that once she got scared, all she wanted was home.

Billy wouldn't think about sleeping either, unless he found

110

a place he considered safe. And no one was home at his house. Where else would he go?

The school!

Connie claimed that school represented a safe haven to many children. Funny time to be thinking about her best friend back in Phoenix. Connie was always laughing over the exploits of the kids in her class. Izzy stuffed her hands in her pockets and walked briskly toward Mayhill Elementary. She didn't turn into its parking lot though, for others had had the same idea, and a kaleidoscope of beams bounced over the playground. The principal stood at the front door talking to Officer Rowe.

For a brief moment, Izzy contemplated yanking on Officer Rowe's sleeve and suggesting they contact Billy's friends, but no doubt, they'd done that. Izzy thought back to the days she'd watched over Billy. What had they done? Where had they gone? The McKenna farm was probably being scrutinized. Where else could he be? Without conscious thought, Izzy headed for the library. A bitter Nebraska wind followed her progress, sending chills down her neck and keeping her pace hurried. She stuffed her hands in her pockets, wishing she'd worn gloves.

The silence of Mayhill Park greeted her. Maybe she should go inside the library and call Francine to see if Billy had returned home yet. It would feel good to spend a moment in the library and out of the chill. Izzy stood, shivering, staring at the dark trees and blowing leaves. She could hear someone on a microphone in the distance, calling Billy's name. The wind increased. She closed her eyes, picturing Billy playing while Delta watched over him. When she opened her eyes, she stepped off the sidewalk and traversed the grass. The old, gnarled tree stood ominously in the middle of the park. She looked up into the towering tangle of limbs and leaves.

"Billy," she whispered. A few leaves swirled down to brush against her face and made her jump. "Billy." She cleared her throat and said it again. "Billy!"

"I want down, Izzy."

Weak-kneed with relief, Izzy leaned against the tree, sucking in breaths of cool air, calming herself. "Billy! I'm so glad I found you! Can you make it to the bottom branch?"

"No. My pants are ripped, and I'm scared."

Izzy reached up and took hold of the bottom limb and struggled to pull herself up. Her frozen fingers felt stiff against the tree. She managed to wrap both her arms around the branch, but when she attempted to swing her feet up they only went halfway. She tried again, making it a little farther this time. Her feet kicked erratically in the air while her hands tore against the rough surface of the old elm. "I'm coming, Billy."

Looking around, Izzy spied one of the big trash cans. Maybe she could turn it over and use it as a step up. She started walking towards it, but Billy's frantic voice stopped her.

"Don't leave me!"

"I'm not, Billy. I'm going to get the trash can." She hurried across the park. The steel container seared her fingers, as if she'd touched an old metal ice-cube tray. She tugged, trying to twist it around, but a chain held it firmly to the park bench, which was cemented to the ground.

A fingernail broke as she gave one last exasperated pull. "Billy, I'm going to have to go for help."

"No," he called frantically. "Don't leave me."

Izzy looked around. Surely with all the searchers out, someone would be near enough to hear her call. "Help! Over here! I've found him!"

The wind picked up force, blowing hair in her mouth as she screamed. She put her hands on the tree branch again and tried to remember how she'd climbed trees when she was little. This time she grabbed the branch and used the tree trunk to walk her way slowly up and then twisted around so that she straddled the branch. For a moment she held on to the branch as if it were the neck of a horse, trying to regain her balance.

"Izzy, what are you doing?" Parker got there just one minute too late to save her from having to climb.

"Billy's in this tree. He's ripped his pants, and he's scared."

Izzy pushed herself up so she was sitting.

"Billy, you okay?" Parker called.

"I want down. I hafta go to the bathroom. And I'm cold."

Parker stepped closer to the tree and held his hands up for Izzy to lower herself into. She scooted her body, hugging the branch as if it were a lifeline. She wrapped her legs tightly around it and then carefully let herself twist and slide until she was hanging from the branch upside down so that when she landed in Parker's arms, he'd cradle her fall.

She didn't want to drop. Not that she didn't trust him—she did. And she knew that he wouldn't let her fall. It made her feel vulnerable in a different way. She closed her eyes and let go. She landed in his arms easily, and for a moment, the chill of the night disappeared. He hugged her to him, as if she weighed no more than a child. Izzy wanted to wrap her arms around his neck, kiss him, and bury herself in the warmth he represented.

He gently stood her on the ground and pulled off his gloves. "Here, hold these." Grabbing the lowest branch, he pulled himself up without a grunt.

Izzy pulled his gloves on and watched him make his way to the shadow that was Billy.

"Hurry, Parker. I hafta go to the bathroom bad."

Once Parker had Billy in his arm, he scooted down the tree. He carried the boy as easily as he had carried Izzy's cat. When he got to the bottom branch, he handed Billy down. Billy let Izzy help, then jumped to the grass and pressed his knees together firmly. "Izzy, please."

"Can you get in the library?" Parker asked.

Izzy took Billy's hand and hurried him to the back door where she punched in the code and flipped on the light. Billy rushed toward the children's section. Not the closest bathroom, but the one he knew best. Izzy entered the dark main room and leaned against the counter. Parker came right behind her.

"Do I need to dial nine for an outside line?"

"No." Izzy reached behind the counter and got the phone.

While Parker calmed his mother, Billy sang the ABC song in the background.

"I was so scared," Izzy admitted, once Parker hung up.

"Why didn't you call somebody when you found him?"

"Every time I started to walk away he got upset. I yelled for help and then tried to get up to him."

"I heard you." Parker took off his jacket and put it over her shoulders. "What made you think of that tree?"

"I was praying, then I thought about a friend I have in Phoenix who runs a day-care center. Everything clicked. When Billy's at the park, he tries to climb that tree. Delta said it's kinda like a passage into growing up. I knew Billy couldn't make it to Lincoln, or even to the outskirts of town, so I tried to think of a place that would make him feel safe."

Parker calmly touched a finger to her chin. "Billy was easier to rescue than your cat." He urged her face toward him and held her chin. The touch reminded Izzy of safety, and love, and commitment. She thought back to her father. Would Parker—? No, surely not. His eyes were tender for the first time. There was hope! This man wasn't lost. His lips settled on hers.

Izzy leaned into the kiss, savoring the bond between them. Then, she felt a tug at her jacket.

"I'm done." Billy was still shivering.

Izzy figured he was too chilled to comment on catching them kissing. He would probably wait and bring it up when there was a crowd of people around.

"Let's get you home, Buster." Parker picked Billy up and hugged the child to him. "Coming, Izzy?"

The Strickland home glowed with the activity of frenzy. A police cruiser was parked in front. All the neighbors gathered on their front porches, two-stepping to the beat of a cold, October night, while they watched Parker carry Billy in.

"He asleep, Parker?" The strain of rushing back from Lincoln to face the terror of looking for a missing child showed in Francine's eyes.

"Yes, Mom."

The phone chose that moment to shrill. Francine grabbed it quickly, but too late. Billy jerked awake. "Is it Mama?"

Francine had no more informed the caller that Billy was fine and hung up, when another call came. "Billy's going to have a tough time falling asleep." Francine frowned at the phone.

"Leave the phone off the hook," Grant advised.

"That's not fair to the people who are out looking. They've been checking frequently to see if Billy's returned. If they can't get through, they might keep looking. No, honey, I've got to answer the phone. Our friends are worried, too."

Officer Rowe sat in the corner filling out paperwork. "Parker, take the boy to your place. Let him get a good night's sleep."

Parker nodded, "Good idea. He'll be happier out in the country."

"Izzy," Carole added, standing up to tuck a crocheted blanket around Billy's shivering form. "I wonder if you'd mind going along. Billy seems quite taken with you. Maybe you can help keep his mind off his mama for a while."

"Why, Carole, I can go along to Parker's and you—" Francine laid the phone on her shoulder, muting her words.

"Now Francine. . . ," Carole walked over and sat down next to Francine.

Parker let Carole's words fade away. He'd seen her well-placed kick to his mother's shins. Thing was, he was perfectly willing to let Izzy accompany him home. Maybe just for tonight and maybe forever. Tonight when he'd looked up into the tree and seen Izzy clutching the branch for dear life—and a moment later when he'd cradled her in his arms—he'd realized that he'd fight to keep her here in Mayhill. Here with him.

"I'll follow in my car," Izzy insisted.

"I appreciate this." Francine started gathering Billy's belongings. "Poor tyke. His whole world's turned upside down."

❧

Izzy kept Parker's taillights in her sight, muttering scoldings at him for driving much too fast. She pressed down nervously on the gas pedal. *Well,* she thought, *this is probably the only time I'll travel seventy miles an hour without worrying about being stopped for speeding.*

Parker gently lifted Billy from the front seat as Izzy pulled her car in behind his. He waited for her to come alongside him. "Kenny doesn't know what he's missing." Parker's eyes rested on Billy and then speculatingly on Izzy.

"You're right." Izzy started up the steps. She paused in front of the door.

"It's open."

"Oh. Yeah." Izzy felt uncomfortable opening the screen. The living room light glowed a welcome. Brute waited, panting by the coffee table. He started toward them, but a word from Parker changed his mind.

Parker edged her aside as he headed toward a door that opened to a bedroom.

Glancing around the masculine living room, Izzy realized she hadn't really gotten a good look the other day. There were a few feminine touches, but most all the furniture was covered with neat stacks of clothes. He kept a neat house, except for the clothes. Brute sniffed at her feet. Idly, she bent down to scratch behind his ears. She could hear Parker talking to Billy as he undressed the child and helped him to bed.

She moved a stack of shirts off one of his chairs and sat down.

"I pretty much live in the living room." Parker stepped back into the room. "My bedroom's clean. You want to see it?"

"Er, no."

"I put Billy in the spare room. Rhea's kids stay there once in a while." Parker shifted from one foot to the other. "Are you hungry?"

"A little." She really wasn't, but it would be more comfortable sitting at the table, trying to make idle conversation, than it would be sitting on the couch staring at a television that only received three channels. No doubt, reruns from the seventies would be playing. Nothing romantic about them. Izzy bit her lip. She hadn't been this nervous since high school.

"How about ham and eggs?"

"Sounds good."

Parker's kitchen had a gray linoleum floor with a big trapdoor in the middle. The cabinets—except for two at the end, newly refinished—were painted a dingy, peeling white. One didn't close all the way, and Izzy could see the plates and glasses perfectly aligned inside. Brute pranced by his doggy dish, knowing that whatever the master ate, Brute ate.

"They used to keep food down there." Parker stepped hard on the trapdoor.

"I've heard of that."

"I don't go down there very often. The steps are very narrow. I'm thinking I'll enlarge them and turn the room into a cellar."

"That would be nice. There's never enough storage space."

"That's what Julia has—" Parker's voice tapered off. He stared at Izzy as if seeing her for the first time.

"Parker, I can go, if you don't need me here."

"No, please. You're the first date I've had since—"

"This isn't a date."

"No," Parker sighed. "It isn't, but I'd like to take you out. A movie, maybe. Dinner?"

"I don't know." Izzy sat at the scratched, wooden table. "Parker, can I ask you something?"

"Anything."

"What do you think about God?"

Parker turned and cracked eggs into a skillet. The sound of popping and sizzling barely dented a silence so tangible it could almost be touched. "I *don't* think about Him."

The emphasis on the word *don't* gave it away. Izzy rubbed her finger over a deep scratch bearing the initials KL. She tried not to sound too eager, but surely this was an opening. "Did you ever?"

"You are the strangest female. I believe in God. Okay? I

just don't think He has much time for me."

"That's not true!"

"Now's not the time, Izzy."

It was too soon for this conversation. She should have waited. This was why she hesitated at inviting more friends to church. She didn't know the right words. This man carried baggage that she didn't understand. If she had understood, maybe she would have been able to help her dad.

Unfortunately, what haunted Parker was the memory of a deceased wife.

Izzy wished she could remember the words spoken to her by her church family after her father's death. The minister had stayed by her. She remembered that. What had the minister here done? She'd have to find out. Of course, in all honesty, Whip had done more to restore her sense of peace than the minister back in Phoenix had. Since starting her Bible study with her landlord just six months ago, she had learned more about forgiveness and strength than she had the previous twenty-five years of her life.

Izzy stood up and made her way to the guest bedroom. Billy lay curled on his side, thumb in his mouth. Izzy could imagine tucking in her own son or daughter and saying good night in this room. She would paint it blue with a Noah and the Ark scene on the wall.

Leaning back, she let her head rest against the closet door. Why did Parker have to be suicidal? She could deal with anything but that. He didn't act depressed. Not like her. No, she wouldn't think about the past. She'd almost managed to forget about his journal tonight. Until he'd brought up Julia's name.

Billy moaned in his sleep, and Izzy moved closer to put a hand to his forehead. He didn't feel warm.

"He's okay. I took his temperature when I put him to bed."

Izzy jumped. "I didn't hear you walk in. I know, poor little guy."

"He's had a rough week, that's for sure."

The phone rang. Parker picked one of the stuffed animals off the floor and laid it next to Billy before leaving the room.

Izzy followed, listening to his one-sided conversation.

"Yeah, everything's okay. . . He's here. . . Delta's gonna be fine. . . Izzy's here, too. . . You're kidding! Carole did. . . I'll tell Izzy."

"What is it?" Izzy asked when Parker hung up the phone.

"It was Robert. They've taken Carole to the hospital in Lincoln. Seems she's been in labor for hours and didn't bother to tell anyone."

"She's so excited." Izzy studied a picture of a much younger Parker, standing between his parents, wearing a sailor's outfit. "I think it's neat she's getting a chance for a second round of motherhood."

"Yeah." Parker didn't look convinced.

Izzy took a deep breath, inhaling the smell of ham. "You think the food's ready?"

"I'm sure it is." Parker led the way to the kitchen.

Izzy followed more slowly. She would eat even if the eggs were runny, and then she'd go. The room was so charged with emotion that she couldn't think of a word to say. She hated feeling ill at ease. He made her so aware. It wasn't fair. She'd never been at a loss for words just because of a man's presence. She almost couldn't breathe.

"You want ketchup?"

"Of course." Izzy sat gingerly at the rickety table and tried not to notice the creaking sounds the chair made as it adjusted to her weight.

"Be careful. That chair belonged to my great-grandma. I never sit in it. Afraid to."

"It belonged to Rosemary?"

Parker raised his eyebrow. "That's right. Tomorrow morning, take a look at the brass bed Billy's sleeping in. It belonged to Rosemary, too."

Izzy rubbed her fingers along the edge of the table.

"Don't get too mushy," Parker warned. "The table used to

belong to Edna." Parker set down two plates of food and sat across from her. Izzy picked up her fork and started rearranging her food.

"You cut the ham up in little pieces and mixed it into the eggs." Izzy stared at her plate.

"It's easier that way. I already had the sharp knife."

"This is the way I eat my ham and eggs." Izzy reached for the ketchup bottle.

Parker got it first and squirted a healthy amount on his eggs. He held the bottle just out of reach. "It will cost you."

"What?"

"Yep, you want the ketchup, I get a date to the movies."

"You like ketchup on your eggs?" Izzy croaked.

"Sure, change the subject. As for the ketchup, I know, it's weird."

"No, it's not. I like it, too. And I'll think about the movie."

Parker grinned, as if they shared some secret and handed the bottle to her without making her promise a movie. "You know," he said. "I think I knew you were going to be a problem when you drove out here to tell me I still owed the library two dollars."

"A problem?" Izzy whispered.

Parker nodded, then said, "I don't want you to be in my thoughts. I don't want to worry about you. But that kiss at the library. . .the one Billy interrupted. Izzy, I want to kiss you again."

"Parker, you don't know me." Izzy felt the world spin out of control. She had daydreamed about this moment. Now it was happening. This couldn't be happening.

He looked into her eyes.

Izzy's skin tingled. He looked so sincere.

"I want to know you," he continued. "Tell me you're not seriously considering returning to Phoenix. You're happy here, aren't you?"

"I'm happy, but—"

"I didn't think I'd ever feel this way again." Parker put his fork down. "After Julia died, I thought I'd spend the rest of my days alone."

Izzy picked up the glass of milk Parker had put in front of her. Idly holding it in front of her, she stared at it, watching the bubbles foam against the rim.

"Are you all right?"

"Parker, when did all this come about?"

"I don't know. I saw you in the library, and then when you kept driving by the fire station. I thought you were crazy. The night you screamed and scared Mark Dalton away, I thought you needed protection. Then, you brought that stupid meat loaf over."

"Parker, I don't know what you want."

"Why? Do you have a boyfriend back in Phoenix?"

"No."

"Then, why?"

Izzy pushed her plate away. "Parker, how well do you know my mother?"

"I like Clara. I even visited her in the hospital in Lincoln when she had her first heart attack. That was before you moved down here."

"You've never talked to her about my. . .dad?"

"No. Why?"

Izzy's cheeks felt as if the air of the room had suddenly been sucked out, leaving nothing left in the atmosphere for her to breathe.

"Izzy, what is it?" Parker put his hand over hers.

"I—" She pulled her hand out from under his. "Ah, Parker, my father killed himself six years ago."

Sympathy shone from his eyes. He put his hand back on hers and leaned forward. "Izzy, I'm so sorry. That must have been hard. Do you know why?"

Izzy blinked. Parker acted as if suicide was a surprising thing, a thing that happened to others. She felt saliva pool in the back of her throat. Suddenly, it was hard to breathe. "I've got to go!" Izzy jumped up, her legs catching the edge of the chair and knocking it over. She backed up, her foot tangling in the chair leg, and she went to the floor on one knee.

Parker's strong hand caught her at the elbow and guided her back up. "Izzy, you need to talk. Have you been holding all this in? Does your mother know you're still upset?"

"Leave me alone, Parker." The tears dripped into her mouth, the salty flavor closing her throat even more. She rushed through the living room, grabbing her purse and tripping down the front steps to her car.

He watched as her taillights bounced out of sight. Whew. Of all things, he hadn't expected her to fall apart on him.

"Parker!" Billy's voice, terrorized, came from the bedroom.

"I'm here," Parker yelled.

Billy was sitting up, sweat dripping down his forehead, the stuffed animal clutched tightly in his arms. "I heard something. I want Izzy."

I want her, too, thought Parker, but didn't say it. "She had to go home."

"What day is tomorrow?"

"Well, I think the tomorrow you're asking about is already today. But, it's Sunday."

"Oh." Billy frowned. "We've been going to Sunday school. Afterwards, can we drive to Lincoln to see Mama?"

"I don't know, Billy. We'll have to see how everyone's schedule looks. What we can do is call your mama's room and see how everything's going. See if she's strong enough to see you. It wouldn't make much sense to drive all the way there, if she was sleeping."

"I wouldn't mind. I can watch my mama sleep."

"I know you would, Buster. You're a good boy."

Parker sat on the edge of the bed and took Billy's hand. Young fingers curled around Parker's thumb, and he felt Billy relax. Parker stayed until the boy's steady breathing signaled sleep.

Pulling his shirt over his head, Parker walked to the living room. He tossed the shirt in the corner. It landed on top of the clothes Izzy had stacked there. She'd only been in his house an hour and already it felt better. He could help her. He knew what it felt like to lose somebody. It just took time to get over the loss, but friendship and love were the best medicines.

Man, Parker thought, listen to me. *I'm telling myself the same things that everybody told me after Julia died.*

Izzy hid it well. He'd never have guessed she was carrying that much grief around and for so long. Parker stripped down to his boxers and sat on the couch, pulling the blanket off the back and starting to cover himself.

For a moment he lay there with the room closing in on him. He stood. If he was going to help Izzy get over her loss, he'd better start working on his own. The first thing he could do was start sleeping in his bedroom again. On the bed he'd shared with Julia.

❧

Whip sat on the front porch. Agatha Hepfield waited next to him.

"Some excitement today, eh, Izzy?" Agatha rocked her chair forward so that she looked past Thompson and at Izzy.

"Enough excitement for me." Izzy nodded, knowing that her red eyes would be blamed on the weather.

"You like little Billy?" Agatha grinned wickedly.

"He's a good kid," Izzy agreed.

"Takes after Parker," Whip said. "Although, technically, I guess Parker's more like a second cousin twice removed, or something. Maybe he's a first cousin, once removed."

Izzy didn't want to hear about Parker. She said good night and went inside. Whip had laid out a piece of pie for her. She grabbed it and a soda before climbing the stairs to her apartment. Radar curled around Rosemary's journal, deep in slumber. Izzy changed into her pajamas and collapsed on the couch, but she was soon scooting up and switching the light back on. She couldn't sleep, so she might as well read. Purposely, she pushed Parker's image away. This time she took the newer-looking journal and got comfortable.

Radar settled on her stomach. His footsteps dug into her chest, making her gasp.

One thing for sure, Izzy decided after rearranging Radar and reading two pages, this journal didn't belong to Rosemary. The first date recorded was in the 1980s. No name decorated the front. Izzy decided to read a little farther before putting it away. The handwriting looking vaguely familiar.

At first, all the entries spoke of school, baseball, catching snakes. Izzy squinted. She wasn't reading the best handwriting. The little boy who'd written this, and it had to be a young boy, because no girl she knew got such joy out of scaring her mother with a snake, certainly wasn't gifted in the art of forming letters.

The boy didn't write every day. According to the dates, he'd write for a couple of days and then put the journal away for a month or more. Izzy skimmed to the middle of the books. It took her into the boy's future, to about 1981. The boy wrote about not liking school, about liking girls, and about having to work part-time at the McKennas' farm. Izzy felt prickles go up and down her arms. Was she reading Parker's journal? She really should stop, she told herself. *One more,* she decided, *I'll just read one more page.*

She turned to the next entry, surprised to discover the boy changing to a slanting cursive. Of course, the date recorded was 1989. The boy wrote about his cousin Parker leaving for college and about his buying a gun.

She wasn't reading Parker's journal—she was reading Kenny's journal. And the handwriting matched the handwriting of the journal Parker had turned into the library. The journal with the entry about suicide.

Izzy felt the pie stick in her throat.

Parker wasn't suicidal.

Kenny was.

ten

Izzy could see the hazy, white sun from her bedroom window, but wasn't sure it radiated any life. Or maybe *she* didn't radiate any life. A sleepless night, a nagging suspicion that she had been irrevocably wrong about Parker, and a yearning for morning to put things right had tormented her thoughts. She dressed quickly, grabbing a soda and trying to blink away fatigue. She put on her coat, tucked her hands into mittens, and wrapped a scarf around her neck. Time to face the music. Shivering, she jumped in the car. The heater hummed, almost drowning out the Christian radio station. Izzy drove, blowing white air into the atmosphere, wondering if she could make a smoke ring with the visible chill. Nebraska was one cold state.

She'd been so wrong about Parker. She had believed that he was suicidal! If he slammed the door in her face, she'd understand. She'd sit on his front porch and cry, but she'd understand. This whole relationship, or nonrelationship, was crazy.

Izzy hit the steering wheel with the palm of her hand. Love wasn't supposed to be this hard. She had prayed for a Christian man who would be her spiritual mate. Instead, she was in love with a torn, rugged fireman who believed in God but didn't follow the faith. The car hit a huge hole in the dirt road. Her purse bounced to the floor. Yeah, here she was driving through the crooked country roads of a community she'd sworn she wouldn't settle in, heading toward the house of the man she wanted to marry.

She'd thought she'd turned everything over to God. But the last few days only proved that she'd kept a piece for herself. It wasn't her fault that her father hadn't been strong enough to face devaluation in the work place. Money had been the cause for ruin of so many men. Look what it had done to Judas.

Often, Izzy thought as her car cruised by the waving branches of tall trees, she'd felt remiss about her religion. So many of her friends accepted God without qualms. Izzy had a problem accepting perfect peace. She tended to let things worry her. Parker was probably a lot like that.

His house looked deserted, with a grayish bitter wind sending the last of October's leaves tumbling across the porch. In the distance, a rooster heralded the morning. Izzy stepped out of the car and slowly made her way to the front door. Clutching her coat closed with one hand, she rang the doorbell.

Parker answered almost immediately, hopping up and down on one foot while holding his boot in his hand. "Izzy?"

"I've got something to tell you. Do you have a minute?"

"I wish I did. The station just called. With everything that's going on, they're shorthanded. I was just getting ready to wake Billy."

He hopped away from the door.

"Parker, I've treated you unfairly." Izzy trailed after him.

"I won't argue." He grinned.

Izzy felt the blush start at her neck and travel to her cheeks. She followed him. "No, I don't mean that. Do you remember the day you turned in all the books at the library?"

"Sure. That's the day I met you." His eyes turned a frosted brown as he took in her padded appearance. "Hand me your coat?"

With nervous fingers, Izzy jerked off her mittens and unbuttoned her coat. Unwrapping the scarf, she tossed it and the rest of her wraps onto a chair. She felt herself melting as he slowly started scrutinizing her from head to toe. She cleared her throat and tried to go on. "Parker do you remember that book I returned to—"

The phone rang. Parker picked it up. Izzy sat down on the couch to wait.

"Mother. . .really? I've got to go to work. Hold on a minute." He turned to her. "Would you be willing to stay with Billy for a little while this morning? Mom's not feeling well."

"Sure," Izzy said, thinking she'd do anything to smooth over what she was about to confess. "I'll watch him. I'll take him to church with me."

"No problem, Mom, Izzy's going to stay with him. Why don't you just call here later this afternoon when you start to feel better, and Izzy will bring him over. Okay, bye."

As soon as he hung up, Izzy said, "Parker, what I was trying to say—"

Static filled the room, then the clear sounds of Robert Parrish barking out orders from the squawk box on top of the television. Parker quickly responded. "Strickland here. I'm on my way."

"Parker, about that journal."

"Izzy, I wish I could stay and talk, but there's a three-car pileup over by the Waco Turnpike. I've got to get to the station. I promise, the moment I can, I'll call you and we'll meet for lunch or something." Then, as if it were a habit, he leaned down and kissed her good-bye—on the lips.

He was out the front door before Izzy could say another word. She fought the urge to touch her mouth.

"Wait," she called after him.

He turned, zipping his coat and pulling on his gloves. "What?"

"I need a key."

He looked quizzical as he opened the car door and started to step up into his truck.

"To your house," she finished.

"No, you don't," he laughed, his chuckles sending white puff rings into the air. "Just close the door. No one will bother anything."

The wind caught at his hair, Izzy held the wooden door and kept it from blowing all the way open. "Parker! I'm going to pray for those people who had the accident and you. Be careful."

He touched his brow in a two-fingered salute, slammed his

door shut, and sped down the winding road.

Izzy closed the door behind her and went to check on Billy. He felt a little warm, but slumbered peacefully. Brute lay cushioned between Billy's legs. Idly, Izzy scratched the dog between the ears. Suddenly, all the events from the night overcame Izzy. Her shoulders sagged and her eyes felt dry. She went back into the living room and looked at the couch. Feeling a little daring, she turned to the open door that led to Parker's bedroom.

It was a big room with only a bed in it. Clothes were folded and stacked on the floor.

He needed a woman.

No, he needed a maid.

Izzy went to the pile of shirts lying on the windowsill. Plucking one off the top, she held it up, considering. She had more than three hours to kill before church. Billy was asleep. She unsnapped her pants and kicked them off before shrugging out of her shirt. She slipped his button-down shirt over the top of her head and crawled into bed. Into Parker's bed. The scent of him wove a spell around her, and she fell asleep with a contented smile on her face.

꒰ꙫ꒱

Parker whistled as he drove back to Mayhill. Robert and he had arrived at the accident just as the car fire was dying down. The state police had restricted the area. Parker had sent the ambulance on its way. It carried the injured, fortunately none seriously hurt. Parker thought briefly about Izzy's comment concerning prayer for this couple. Nah, that couldn't have made a difference. After thoroughly dousing the smoldering vehicle, the firemen turned their engine toward home. Mayhill waited just five miles ahead. Already Parker could see the grain towers like a lighthouse beacon welcoming him home.

"You're looking good this morning, Parker," Robert teased. "Wife said Carole Martin sent Izzy out to your house last night to help with the kid. Could it be she stayed all night?"

"No," Parker said, "she didn't stay all night. Izzy's not like that." Then, laughing at the disappointed look on Robert's face, he added, "But she did come back this morning."

"Finally!" Robert exclaimed. "Ty and Jeff have been after me the last few weeks with all sorts of ideas to help fix you two up, but I told them you didn't need any help."

"I'm going to marry her, Robert. Just as soon as I can." Parker started coughing, his own words surprising him.

Robert threw back his head and howled with laughter. "You Stricklands always did make up your minds quickly. Izzy's a fine girl."

"I told her I'd meet her for lunch today. That okay?" Parker felt a sweat breaking out on his forehead as he realized the implications of what he was saying.

"She'll have to come to the station. Jeff and Ty have been at the job forty-eight hours straight. I sent them home. It's just you and me, and I have a pile of paperwork. With this weather, I'd rather have you stick near the radio."

"That's fine. Izzy won't mind."

Robert rolled down the window and stuck his head out into the cold. The wind sent his hair flying back, and the chill from the outside seeped around Parker.

"It's a good thing they took Carole into Lincoln last night," Robert yelled. "They've been predicting our first storm, say it's going to arrive within the next twenty-four hours."

"I love the first snow of the season." Parker smiled as the image of Izzy standing at his front door bundled into winter wraps crossed his mind. He tugged on Robert's sleeve, bringing his boss back into the truck. Then he paused. He used to love the first snow. He'd hated the snow since Julia died. Could it be he was finally looking forward to winter?

Robert left his hand outside for a few moments, fingers spread. "This one feels different. Like it's going to be a whiteout."

Parker didn't like the worried expression on Robert's face. His boss seldom tried to predict occurrences, but it seemed as if Robert was filled with concerns today. Come to think of it, pulling a forty-eight straight really wasn't that tough. Why was Robert so concerned about Jeff and Ty?

Mayhill was waking up as Parker and Robert drove back into town. The line at the fast food restaurant was forming as people stopped to get their one-minute breakfast. Parker saw the minister of Izzy's church drive by as Robert pulled into the station. Parker checked over the engine while Robert went inside to file a report.

The police call came in at eleven. Parker relayed it over the station radio. . .a barn fire on route five. . .man injured. . .hay. Robert drove this time. Parker called his house from the truck's phone as they sped back in the direction of the earlier car fire. He expected to leave a message, sure that Izzy was at church. Instead, she answered.

Parker liked the thought of her answering his phone. "Lunch is off. Did I wake you?"

"No," she sound distracted.

"Izzy, is something wrong?"

"Billy's feverish. What should I do?"

"Give him plenty of fluids. Keep him in bed. Don't let him walk on the bare floor. We're responding to a call. It could be a while. I'll phone you when it's over. If he gets worse, take him into to town to my mother."

"Okay."

"Izzy," Parker lowered his voice, knowing Robert was listening. "I love you." His throat constricted on the words.

"I think I love you, too."

He let out his breath. "We'll work on that *think* part," Parker promised. "Bye."

Parker set the phone down.

"Your mother's not sick, you know?" Robert said.

"What do you mean Mom's not sick?"

"Whip spread the word that Izzy came back home disheartened last night. Carole was sure upset that her plan to get you two talking didn't work. But then this morning Agatha saw Izzy leave, heading in your direction, and called your mother.

Your mother called Jeff." Robert took a deep breath, exaggerating his commentary. "Jeff knew you were being called in and decided that there's was no better way to get you two acting like a couple than to put you in charge of Billy."

"That's ridiculous."

"You still sleeping on the couch?"

"I didn't last night."

"Okay, then I'll tell Ty, Jeff, Carole, Agatha, Whip, Rhea, and your mother that you don't need any more help." Robert made a big production out of counting off his fingers at the recital of each name.

If Parker had been driving, he'd have put his head down on the wheel and moaned. "You're really enjoying—"

"Look," Robert pointed, suddenly animated, "no wonder York radioed for help."

Black swirls of smoke billowed toward the clouds and blended into the sky. Robert steered the fire engine a safe distance from the burning barn and jumped out. Parker ran around to the back and hooked his arm into the coils of hose. Running toward the action, Parker felt the first wave of heat hit his cheeks with stinging tentacles of airborne fire.

"Didn't expect to see you all so soon," one of the York firefighters yelled. Jeff and Ty pulled up in Jeff's car. Jeff joined Parker.

"Gonna be one of those days! Luckily, this is the old barn. The farmer built a new one and was just feeding out of this one. There's not much hay inside," reported a York fireman.

"Thank God," Parker murmured. He hated burning hay. "Anybody hurt?"

"Farmer took quite a knock to the head. He was out here caring for the stock. Says he heard something and when he went to check it out, interrupted a man going through an old desk he keeps in the tackroom."

"Wife home?" Robert yelled.

"No, she's shopping in town. We have an officer looking for her."

The York fireman relieved Parker of the hose. Parker joined Ty and a group of men busy breaking open bales of hay to scatter them so they could be doused thoroughly.

"Good time for it to snow," Robert yelled from behind them.

Parker nodded as he watched his chief hurry over to the pond where York's engineer was readying a hose for suction.

"Parker?"

"What, Mike?"

"Just thought you'd better know. The farmer gave a good description of the man who probably started the fire."

Parker felt the water pressure easing as the engine emptied. "So?"

"It sounds like your cousin Kenny. Sheriff's put out an APB."

"Kenny! You sure?"

"If I wasn't sure, I wouldn't tell you, Parker. You might want to get to your aunt Edna as soon as you can."

"And the troopers have already been called?" Parker asked.

"Arson's a serious offense."

❧

Izzy came awake with the graceful yawn of a woman content. She hugged Parker's pillow to her face and drank in his scent. His bed. She'd spent the night, well really the day, in his bed. Rolling out of bed she tugged on her jeans before going to check on Billy. He slumbered on. Izzy felt his forehead again. He was still a little warm.

"Billy." She shook his shoulder.

"Wha–at," he grumbled.

"You hungry?"

He fell back asleep before he could answer.

Padding silently through Parker's house in her stocking feet, Izzy felt so thankful she could almost purr. Izzy let the dog out, filled his bowl with dry dog food, and shook her head at the dimming skies. How had she slept past suppertime? Amazing. The search for Billy, combined with worry about Parker, must have been more taxing than she realized. She had her work cut out for her, now, that was for sure. Opening the bottom cupboards, she found Parker's supply of soup and grabbed a can of chicken broth.

"I'm not hungry," Billy mumbled when she woke him up.

"You need to eat."

"How's my mom?"

"Tell you what," Izzy promised, "you eat half this soup, and we'll call her."

Billy winced, but obediently pushed himself to a sitting position and weakly took the bowl of soup from Izzy's hands. "Half?"

"Half," Izzy said.

Parker's clothes were still in the corner where she'd tossed them last night. Izzy gathered them up and went looking for the washer and dryer. She tried the bathroom in Parker's bedroom first. Next, she went out to the garage. Last, she investigated the back porch. Surely the man owned a washer and dryer. Shrugging, she headed back to check on Billy. He managed to maintain his upright position, but his head was nodding dangerously close to the soup. Izzy relieved him of the bowl and started to tuck him in. The wet spot of soup on his T-shirt stopped her.

"Billy, wake up."

"Izzy, I don't feel good." He shivered.

"I know. Your shirt's wet. Let's just take it off and then you can go back to sleep. By the way, where's Parker's washer and dryer?"

"At the fire station. He showed me," Billy mumbled.

"He doesn't have a washer and dryer here?"

"In the basement."

"Basement?" She didn't remember any basement.

"Yeah, you know, where they used to keep canned goods. That's where we keep ours."

Ah, the cellar. "Oh." She tucked the covers up over Billy's shoulders and went back to the kitchen. Looking at the floor, she located the handle that lay flat in a slight indentation on the floor. Izzy bent, grabbed it with a firm hand, and tugged upward as hard as she could. It resisted, and she pulled harder. The metal handle dug into her hand. Izzy almost gave up, but now she was curious. It took two broken nails and more than five minutes, but she finally managed to open the trapdoor.

The steps went straight down, a ladder effect instead of gradual descent. As her foot touched the ground, the idea of a flashlight came to her and she climbed back up. She found Parker's flashlight in a kitchen drawer, next to a pair of rolled-up socks and an empty aluminum foil box.

A chill followed her down the steps. As her foot touched the ground for the second time, she began to doubt the need to do Parker's laundry. He probably did it at the station house. They had a washer and dryer there. And she seemed to recall Parker saying he didn't come down here much. Well, he didn't do laundry much, so that didn't mean anything. She swung the flashlight around and squinted in the darkness trying to detect some type of light switch.

Instead, the flashlight beam found the leering face of Kenny Latkam.

&

It was growing dark, but the fire was out. Parker grimly held the heavy hose, fatigued beyond belief. This time his cousin had gone too far. Not Parker, nor Edna, nor Mayor Martin would be able to ease Kenny through with only another misdemeanor on his record. Arson was a serious crime, and not one society could afford to ignore, even if the guilty party happened to be a hometown boy.

Parker wiped the sweat from his brow and noticed Robert's worried gaze. His boss's predictions had come true once too often today. The snow that fell from the sky gathered on the ground quickly, and already the firemen's footsteps could be seen.

"We're finished up here, Parker," Robert called.

This time York had the bulk of the paperwork. Numbly, Parker hopped into the front seat, closing his eyes and letting his head fall against the seat cushion.

"Robert, do you think it was Kenny?"

"You know it was."

"I don't think Kenny would set a fire."

"I doubt Kenny meant to. Still, if the boy wasn't trying to rob the farmer in the first place, he wouldn't have been near the barn. Chances are, Kenny dropped his cigarette as he tried to run."

"Do you think—?"

"I think it's time Kenny faced up to his troubles. There's not a thing you can do this time, Parker. Probably would have been better if Kenny had faced the music a long time ago."

"But Aunt Edna—" Parker began.

"Spared the rod and spoiled the child," Robert finished.

"Did you know Kenny was Billy's father?"

"I was one of the few."

"How long have you known?"

"Since Billy was born. You remember Delta's senior year, don't you?"

"Not really."

"That's right," Robert gripped the steering wheel. "You were newly married, living up in Lincoln. Delta kicked up quite a stir. She didn't keep a steady boyfriend, but went out with them all. She went out with Jeff, Mark Dalton, your cousin Chris from over in Waco. Her dad was fit to be tied. He'd ground her, she'd sneak out the window. Twice she disappeared for a week, only to turn up at her parents' doorstep, refusing to tell where she'd been or who'd she'd been with."

"How do you know all this?"

The knuckles on the steering wheel turned white. "She dated Russ."

Parker stared ahead, knowing how hard it must have been for Robert to admit that his son had been involved with Delta during that time.

"We were worried that Billy might belong to Russ," Robert went on, eyes fixed on the road. "I was there when Billy was born. It was in January. Delta went into labor, and they were headed toward Doc's when the car skidded in the snow and went into a ditch. We got her to the emergency room in time. I happened to be nearby when Delta mumbled his name. I didn't say anything. If Delta wanted the father to know, she'd announce it. Fact is, she was smart not to. Having Kenny for a father will be a millstone around that boy's neck.

"The town spent a few months speculating on whose baby Billy was: Chris, Russ, Mark, Kenny. Finally folks settled on Chris. Kenny didn't pay any attention to Billy. Chris was the logical choice. He went off to college in Texas and never came back. Delta didn't deny it. The few of us who knew let sleeping dogs lie."

Parker shook his head. "What a mess."

"Parker, you don't think Edna would help Kenny get away?"

"Not once she knows arson's involved. She's pretty shook about him being Billy's father and her not knowing she had a grandson all these years."

The snow swished off the windshield and the two men finished the rest of the journey into town in silence.

⁊⦁

The flashlight hit the ground and rolled. Kenny quickly picked it up and idly tossed it from one hand to the other. "Nice shirt."

Izzy backed up, feeling the wooden beams of the steps dig into her shoulder blades. In the shadowed basement Kenny looked bigger. She had never met the esteemed cousin Chris, but Kenny looked like a smaller, somewhat-erased version of Parker. Tonight he looked as if he had been stepped on, beaten, and thrown away. His white T-shirt was streaked with dirt, and the bottom of his pants were torn and still wet. "What are you doing down here, Kenny?"

"I just wanted a little peace and quiet. What are you doing down here?"

Izzy glanced around. No washer or dryer. She should have known that. Parker had said he planned on redoing the cellar. "Oh, Billy said the washer and dryer were down here." Quickly, Izzy turned and put her foot on the first narrow step.

Kenny came up behind her. The scent from his body seemed tangible: cigarettes and fear, with a chaser of alcohol. Together they climbed to the kitchen.

"What are you going to do, Kenny?"

"They won't be looking for you. You're going to drive me out of here."

"What are you talking about?" Izzy looked out the kitchen window, hoping more than anything that she'd see Parker's truck pull in.

"We'll go to Denver." Kenny didn't answer her question.

Izzy clamped her lips shut and glared. Inside, her brain went into overdrive. *Lord,* she prayed, *what's happening? What should I do? Please, please, keep us safe. Don't let him hurt Billy.*

Kenny only chuckled. He went into the living room, heading with a sense of self-assurance that let Izzy know that while she'd been sleeping he'd been going through the house—and maybe even her purse.

With one halting step, Izzy moved toward the back door. The prayer had made her feel better, but not completely safe. She could do this. Billy was the most important factor. She had a spare car key in a magnetic box hidden up under the front grill. All she had to do—

"You wouldn't leave me alone with Billy," Kenny called.

Izzy froze. "Why not?"

"I've had a lot to drink. Oh, and if I hear you even go near the phone, I won't let you pack."

"What! Kenny, what's going on? What's wrong with you? This isn't funny—"

"Shut up!"

Billy came, sleepy-eyed, to the doorway of the bedroom. "What's he doing here, Izzy?"

"Come on, Billy. We're going to—"

"You're going to do nothing but what I tell you to do," Kenny yelled.

Sitting down on the couch, Izzy beckoned for Billy to join her. Kenny ran into Parker's bedroom, but immediately stuck his head out the door, "Don't even think about moving." A few minutes later he came back in the room carrying a pillowcase bulging with clothes. He began opening cupboards and stuffing food into the corners. "Grab whatever you want for the kid. You've got two minutes and then we're out of here."

Izzy slowly stood, wanting to run but afraid to move. "Billy, just stay where you are." She wanted to show him she wasn't afraid. Taking one step in Kenny's direction, she said, "Why are you doing this?"

"It's time I got away. A small town suffocates you, especially when your whole family oohs and aahs over Parker and Chris. I wasn't fast enough for the football team, I wasn't tall enough for basketball, but I could hold my liquor. I'm not the kid's father, no way, no how. Delta was with Chris before she was with me. Nothing's ever been fair around this place. We'll get to Denver, you'll see. No one's going to stop us. Not while we got the kid."

Izzy backed up. The overpowering odor of whiskey suddenly pushed her into the realization that Kenny was out of control. She'd seen drunk before, and Kenny was about a quart beyond that.

"I'll go to Denver with you, but I don't think we should take Billy. The kid will just get in the way."

For a moment Kenny looked thoughtful, then he frowned at her. "The McKennas are rich. They'll pay a ransom for Billy."

"Billy's your son, Kenny!"

"Well, then my mom will probably fork out some money, too. You're wasting time. You've got one minute to get your stuff together."

Izzy ran for the living room, plopping down in the chair and cramming her feet inside her boots. Shoving her arms through her coat sleeves, she tried to think rationally. They'd have to stop for gas somewhere. She'd get Billy out of the car—

"Come on!" Kenny came out of Billy's room, holding the terrified boy tightly and scowling. "I have nothing to lose, Izzy. Don't even think about leaving me alone with Billy."

"I'm not thinking about leaving you. I'm wondering if we should grab some blankets. It's supposed to snow tonight."

"Get the blankets. Now!"

With a handful of covers, Izzy stumbled after Kenny. She was sure there had to be a way out of all this, but for the life of her she couldn't think of what it was. Billy was using both hands to try to push himself away from Kenny. Tightening his grip, Kenny ignored the terror in Billy's eyes and opened the car door.

"Let me drive, Kenny." Izzy wanted to hit him.

"I don't think so. You learn some pretty neat things in boot camp. I especially enjoyed the survival games. Got really good at tying knots." With a wicked grin, he pulled some rope out of his jacket pocket. Roughly, he wrapped it around Izzy's wrists before winding it about Billy's. He shoved them in the front seat, wound the rope between the door handle, and slammed and locked the car door before climbing behind the wheel.

"Don't even think about gas stations or fast food joints. In the time it would take you to get that knot undone, if you could manage that, I'd be back. You're with me now, and nothing's changing that."

"Kenny, it's starting to snow." Izzy's fear made her voice crack.

With a rebel yell, Kenny turned the key and pressed the Peugeot's gas pedal to the floor. "I like driving in the snow."

As the car skidded down the gravel driveway, Izzy shot a quick glance back at Parker's disappearing house. With a sinking heart, she realized that in Kenny's drunken state, it was very doubtful they'd make it to anywhere near Denver.

eleven

Edna had married well. Each time Parker pulled into the circular driveway he felt as if he were visiting somebody else's aunt. Today, the house had a neglected look to it. Like lost party favors, newspapers littered the sidewalk in front of the door. Leaves covered the basin of the decorative fountain. The chiseled, white, ceramic angel no longer spewed liquid in the air and seemed to shiver from the cold. Usually Edna's house qualified as a showplace. Not today.

Parker left his truck in front of the triple garage, and shoving his hands into his pockets, slowly walked to the front door. Too often he'd been the one to bring Aunt Edna bad news. When he was younger, she'd called him a tattletale and closed the door in his face. Later, during his teenage years, it had been his fault that Kenny often had to be left on the front step, too drunk to find his house key. It didn't matter whether Parker had been with his cousin or not. He was older and always received the blame.

Raising the antique knocker, Parker dropped it, three times. No one answered.

Edna had to be home. It was Sunday night, late. Leaving the step, Parker walked around to the backyard and peeked in a window at a dark kitchen. "I don't believe this," Parker mumbled. The first gnawing tendrils of worry surfaced as he hastened back to his truck to retrieve Edna's spare house key from the glovebox.

The house had at one time belonged to a wealthy rancher. He'd built the clapboard home to impress the wife he'd ordered from the East. There were more rooms than necessary and enough open space to confuse a family of mice. It never felt quite like a home to Parker, more like a museum.

He found his aunt in her late husband's den, huddled at the desk and shaking.

Edna had always been high-strung. Parker wondered how long this anxiety attack had been going on.

"Parker." Edna took a long breath, it looked painful. She stood up and started to pace. "Things will be fine in the morning."

For a shocked moment, Parker stood in the middle of the room. Fine? Who was she kidding? Pictures of Kenny and of Dale, her late husband, smiled at Parker from the desk.

Edna might be bossy and overbearing, but she didn't deserve this.

"I'm going to make you some hot tea, Edna. Now, I want you to stop worrying. We'll find Kenny."

Her gray hair, usually efficiently coiled about her round, red face, now hung in limp imitations of shocked steel wool. "I don't know where Kenny is. They kept asking. I just don't know."

Parker stepped back, feeling helplessness mix with anger. With a stiff-legged turn, he headed toward the kitchen and dialed his mother's number. Francine promised she would be there in fifteen minutes. Parker figured more like five.

He dialed his own number next. Izzy was probably frantic with worry. He wanted to hear her voice, have her tell him that everything was fine, and that she had a pot of chili—or something—on the stove, just waiting for his return. He knew what she'd say if he told her about Kenny. She would offer to pray. He would listen. He could do that.

Her earlier prayer—the one about the accident—had been answered.

Maybe he would ask her to pray for Edna, and for Kenny.

A busy signal came from the other end. Well, he'd get back to her later. He glanced at the clock. It was well after eleven. There had been more excitement in Mayhill, the last week, than there had been in the entire last year—make that decade. He added water to the teakettle and turned on the gas stove.

Edna was still shaking when Francine arrived. Parker watched as his mother bent over Edna, talking soothingly as if to a baby, and having her sister sip tea. "Come on, Edna. You just need a nap. Nothing to be ashamed of. Sleep will make you feel better." Francine walked Edna to her bedroom.

Parker remained in the den, tapping his foot on the floor, anxious to leave Edna's house and look for Kenny, to do something physical.

The police would be back in the morning. He was almost surprised that they weren't still here. There was nothing of Kenny's in this room, except the photographs. Edna, although she had a blind eye where Kenny was concerned, had kept charge of the family's holdings. A quick perusal of Kenny's old room added no insights.

He met his mother coming out of Edna's room.

"She awake?" Parked tried to peek into the bedroom.

"No," Francine replied. "But it's not a peaceful sleep, either. Why'd you come here?"

"To see if she would tell me more than she told the state troopers."

Francine's eyebrows shot up. "You don't think she'd lie?"

"No, I don't think she would lie, but I do think she would purposely forget to mention any details they didn't specifically ask."

"I cannot believe Kenny started that fire."

"There's not positive proof, but it doesn't look good."

The phone rang. Francine's mouth hung open, primed to ask more questions. Parker picked up the receiver. "Latkams'."

"Parker!" Robert Parrish's voice boomed over the receiver. "The police have traced Kenny's car to the McKennas' and—"

"Good, I'll be right there."

"Not so good," Robert went on. "Kenny's not there."

"Where do they think. . .?" Parker's voice faltered. He knew where the police would go from McKennas'. They'd go to his house, right next door. The house he'd left just this morning. The house where Izzy and Billy had waited for Francine to call when she felt better. The house with the busy signal.

Parker picked up the phone and called Whip. It took a while, but finally the old man's yawning voice growled an answer. Parker didn't waste time on a salutation. "Have you seen Izzy and Billy?"

"Why, no, I thought they were with you."

Parker muffled the phone against his heart for a moment, then shot off another question. "But you called?"

"Yes, earlier, but the line was always busy."

Francine's eyes brimmed with tears. "Parker, is everything all right? Do you need me to head over—"

"Stay with Edna," Parker shouted, slamming down the phone. "If she wakes up, call Robert!"

The streets were slicking up as Parker frantically attempted to make record time to his house. For a moment he regretted his choice to live so far away from the community. If he'd purchased the house down the street from his mother's, he'd already be home and figuring out what was going on. He hated losing control. It made him vulnerable. Caring for Izzy was making him vulnerable, but also alive. Her with her talk of God, her love for children. Her smile.

Parker sped up as the beginning of his property came into sight. Every light was on, and two cruisers blocked his drive. Not caring if he slid off the road, he floored it and almost hit the back of Officer Rowe's patrol car, parked just inside the drive. Jumping out of the truck he slipped in the snow and started going down. In a flash, Brute was out the front door and jumping against Parker's knees. Catching hold of the car door handle, Parker hauled himself up and hurried toward his front door, with Brute prancing excitedly at his heels.

"Parker," Officer Rowe opened the door, frowning. "We've been looking for you."

"I was at Edna's. Kenny's not there."

"We've traced him here. Why don't you—?"

"Izzy! Billy!" Parker pushed past Rowe and looked inside the guest bedroom. The messed-up bed looked empty and accusing.

Officer Rowe grasped Parker's elbow firmly. "You mean Billy should be here, in the care of Isobelle de la Rosa?"

"They're not here," Parker said brokenly.

Puppy barks came from the kitchen. Parker rubbed his lip, trying to think about what Kenny might have done. The barks continued. Officer Rowe took a notebook out of his shirt pocket and said, "When did you last speak with Izzy?"

"Before noon. I called her while we were heading toward the York fire."

"Did she sound all right?"

Parker held up his hand letting Rowe know he needed a moment to think. Brute wouldn't be announcing his hunger from the kitchen. The puppy would be sinking his teeth into the hem of Parker's pants and dragging his master toward the bowl. "Something's wrong."

Rowe nodded, following Parker to the kitchen. Brute whined and scraped his paw against the floor right above the cellar trapdoor.

"What is it, Brute?" Parker bent down and tugged at the latch. It gave easily, letting Parker know it had been opened recently.

"Let me—" Rowe began, but Parker had already descended.

The glaring light cast shadows around the cobweb-laden cellar. Rowe stepped off the last stair and joined Parker in scrutinizing the small room. Brute barked from the kitchen, clearly wanting to join them but hindered by the steep steps.

"Over there." Rowe nudged Parker in the direction of a stack of old boxes.

A blanket lay on the ground. An empty pack of cigarettes was pushed to one side.

"Kenny's brand." Parker nodded.

Rowe climbed back upstairs. "I'm going to radio this in. Kenny stole a car in Lincoln. Wrecked it a few miles down from the barn he tried to burn. Catherine Wilfong picked him up and dropped him off at Summers this afternoon, probably about the same time you were putting the fire out. Now we know he's been here. It looks as if he was planning to stay for a while, but something interrupted him. I'm willing to bet Izzy stumbled onto to him. What do you think?"

"She drives one of those little Peugeots." Parker pictured the little car, and in his mind's eye, it shrank to child size.

"What did you remember?" Officer Rowe took a small notebook out of his shirt pocket.

"Those cars are lousy in bad weather. Too small." Parker winced as the picture of Izzy's Peugeot came to mind. The little red car could have skidded off the interstate and her body might be slumped across the front seat. Parker didn't waste any more time contemplating. With three steps he was out the front door and running into the darkness.

Rowe raced behind him. "Just what do you think you're doing?"

"He not only has Izzy, he has Billy!" Parker had one foot in the truck, ready to hop in, when a thought came to him. He grabbed his flashlight, stepped down, and hurried over to where Izzy had parked her car that morning. The tracks had been snowed over, but enough of a faint outline remained, evidence that someone had put that car in reverse and backed out at top speed. The fact that he could still see the impression gave him hope. They might have left an hour ago, or if luck was with him, as little as a half hour. Kenny wouldn't go back to Lincoln. He'd already been there and caused enough trouble to be noticed. Besides, Mayhill people loved to visit Lincoln. With all Kenny had done, he needed to go somewhere and get lost. Parker knew Kenny was heading for Denver, heading for Denver in a totally unsuited vehicle. Parker looked back down at the tire tracks.

She was an Arizona girl in a midget car without snow tires, and his idiot cousin was at the wheel.

Parker hurried to his truck. Brute scampered at his heels. Opening the door, Parker leaned against it for a moment, gathering his thoughts. Brute jumped in. Parker finally swung in behind the wheel. He put his hand on the ignition key, paused, then bowed his head to pray.

❧

Kenny took the exit to Grand Island. The town, only an hour from Mayhill, was one Izzy never visited. And in this darkness, she couldn't identify a single distinguishing feature.

Izzy tightened her grip on the door handle and tried to scoot farther away from Kenny. In troubled slumber, Billy nestled closer. Kenny didn't seem to notice.

"Why are we stopping?" Izzy tried not to sound worried.

"Snow's getting worse. Best fill the tank now and try to outrun the blizzard. We're not staying, and you're not getting out of the car. Thanks to the new pay-at-the-pumps systems, I won't even need to go inside the station." Kenny reached in his pocket and extracted her bank card. "I just slide this in, punch a few numbers, and we're done."

"Billy has to go to the bathroom."

"He can hold it."

"I have to go, too."

"Tough."

At that moment, Izzy thought she'd never disliked anyone as much as she did Kenny. She stared out the window and started to pray, but the prayer choked in her throat and became more a plea for help.

The city of Grand Island provided numerous filling stations and restaurants just off the interstate exit. Kenny drove slowly, looking left and right, frowning at the lines of cars pulling into motel parking lots and convenience stores.

"What are you looking for?" Izzy wanted to feel Billy's forehead, but her hands were firmly connected to the door.

"A gas station without any customers."

It took him a few miles, but finally he pulled into a forlorn station toward the downtown section. He parked as far away from the office as possible and reached over to unroll her window.

"Kenny, it's freezing!"

Jumping out of the car, he ran around and pushed her card

into the slot. "What's your pin number?"

"I don't remember."

He grinned mercilessly, and pushed his jacket open just enough to show the butt of a gun. "Number?" he repeated.

Izzy blinked. How could she have figured he didn't have a gun? She remembered reading about it in his journal, and if he was crazy enough to write about suicide, he was probably crazy enough to threaten his own child.

"This isn't funny, Kenny." Izzy straightened up and gave him a stern look. "Untie the rope, now! I'll explain everything to Parker. He can help you."

Kenny glared at her. "I don't want Parker's help. I never did. I can take care of myself and you."

"This is kidnapping. Kenny, do you know what kind of a jail term kidnapping brings?"

Kenny's unruly hair danced wildly in his eyes as he shook his head negatively. "No. Prisons are overcrowded. I'm under the influence and known to be suicidal. A good lawyer will get me off."

"Who will pay for the lawyer—?" She stopped. Edna had the money.

"Give me the pin number."

"Loosen the ropes, and I'll give you the number."

For a moment, she thought he wouldn't do it. Then, he shrugged. She held her breath as he opened the passenger-side door. Cold air swished in. Izzy stiffened. After a few moments of fumbling, Kenny left her right hand tied to the arm rest, but separated her and Billy.

"You bug me," he threatened, "and I tie you even tighter than before."

"Please, leave Billy untied."

Kenny shook his head, but Izzy noticed that he tied Billy's hand in front of him, with a much looser loop. He also moved the boy to the backseat.

She thought about asking if she could move to the backseat, too, but one look at her kidnapper stymied that notion. She gave him the ID number. His bloodshot eyes looked crazed. In his state of mind, he didn't know or care what he was doing. A lawyer would have a strong case.

"Izzy, will we be all right?" Billy mumbled.

"Don't you worry," Izzy comforted. "God has a special angel in the car with us, and he'll make sure nothing bad happens. I've been talking to God since we got in this car. He will take care of us. You talk to Him, too. He'll listen, Billy. This is just a. . .a funny adventure."

"I wish Grandpa would hurry up and come get us," Billy said, staring out the window. "I'm telling God to send him right now."

"Good idea." Izzy didn't really want Thomas McKenna. She wanted Parker, and strangely enough, she expected him. Maybe that was why she wasn't more scared. She heard the nozzle clink against the pump as Kenny finished. The car shook, Izzy turned and looked toward Kenny. He pointed a threatening finger, then looked up and down the street before dashing into the tiny store that ran from the gas station's office.

Izzy looked in the same direction as Kenny had gone. The street was deserted. She stuck her head out the window. A bitter wind scorched her cheeks with ice particles. She opened her mouth, wanting to scream. The wind took the words and flung them right back at her. Tugging at the rope, she fought to untie it, succeeding only in shredding her right hand as the tough rope tore into her skin.

"I told you I tied good knots." Kenny easily slid behind the wheel. He pulled a six-pack out of a brown paper sack, separated a bottle, and twisted the top off. Taking a swig, he added, "Sorry, didn't think about asking you if you wanted anything." He took another long drink and then offered her the open bottle. "You want some of this?"

Izzy managed to gingerly roll up the window. Her hands felt swollen from just the short time she'd wrestled with the rope. Kenny told the truth. He did tie good knots.

"No, I want to go home." Izzy clutched the door handle as

Kenny spiraled the car crazily onto the main street and back toward the interstate.

"Don't you ever shut up?" Kenny's lip went thin with anger. He took another gulp from the bottle and shot Izzy a dirty look.

The snow came down in close-knit clusters of flakes, making it impossible to see more than a few feet ahead. The streets were now completely empty. Izzy envied the wise folks secure in the comforts of their homes, snug in bed. By far, this was the most terrifying event that had ever happened to her. She'd been raised in a home where church and family came first. Money had figured in, maybe a bit too much, especially at the end, but growing up, she had always felt secure. Were there families where alcohol made every day as desperate as this one? Was there really so much of nothing in Kenny's soul, that he would willingly endanger his own child?

"Can we turn the heater on?" Izzy tried to keep her voice steady.

Kenny finished the beer and belched. "I'm not cold." He stuck his hand in the bag and pulled out another bottle.

"Why don't you let me drive? I promise—"

"I know all about women and their promises." Kenny turned back onto I-80, and into the whiteness, beginning to sing off-key.

Izzy looked behind her. They'd just left Grand Island. Thanks to the darkness and snow, all proof that it existed was blocked. The lack of visibility hindered road signs from being seen. Izzy glanced at her watch. Well after two. Maybe Billy would fall asleep. He didn't need to be awake during all this.

"There's a rest stop ahead. Can we please stop?" Izzy said.

Kenny paused between words and seemed to consider. "If there's no one around, I'll stop."

He didn't. Truckers, more sensible than Kenny, had taken over the parking lot and were sleeping away the bad weather.

Kenny started singing in a uneven voice that quickly reverted to off-color songs.

He finished his second bottle and went for a third.

Izzy tried to keep her voice steady. She didn't want Billy picking up on her worry. "Billy, can you put your seat belt on?"

"No."

"Have you tried?"

"No."

"Well, try."

The rope around Izzy's arm tightened, digging in and irritating her already chafed wrist.

"I can't put it on with my hands tied, and I'm cold." Billy sobbed.

"Please try, Billy." Izzy watched as Billy twisted his body up and tried frantically to bring together the two straps. He'd just get one strap where he wanted it, and then he'd lose it when he reached for the connecting belt. "Don't give up. You're doing fine."

"Got it!"

Kenny turned more sullen by the moment. He turned to glare at Billy and opened his mouth to say something, but with his attention off the road, for only that one second, he allowed the vehicle to meander toward the emergency lane. No other cars had traveled over the accumulating snow on the interstate's edge. The Peugeot's tires slid off the road. Izzy screamed. Kenny jerked forward, grabbing the wheel and doing exactly the opposite of what he'd been taught. Instead of going with the spin, he spun the wheel clockwise. The out-of-control car picked up speed and bounced off the pavement and onto the flat land surrounding I-80. The grassy snow didn't slow down progress. Before Izzy could form her second scream, the car went nose down in a ditch, finally stopping. Kenny slumped against the steering wheel, and silence entered the car along with the smell of alcohol and urine.

"Billy, are you all right?"

"I wet my pants."

"That's okay. I almost did, too." Izzy gingerly turned around to look at Billy.

He looked fine, a little white around the edges, but physically unharmed. He had even slipped his hand out of the loosely tied rope. Izzy tugged at her hand, but it was still bound tightly to the door. She felt the blood dribble down her wrist. The impact had caused the rope to tighten, and because the rope wasn't about to give, her skin had.

"Are you bleeding anywhere?" Izzy tried to sit up. She felt weak, but managed to turn around and give Billy a thorough going over.

"Nope. Is he dead?"

Izzy put out two fingers and felt Kenny's neck for a pulse. Touching him made her jumpy, but the steady beat of his heart made her breath easier.

"He's not hurt, he's passed out from the beer. We've got to get out of here." Izzy tried to work at the knot.

"If I was wearing my jeans, I could give you my jackknife."

"That would be good," Izzy agreed. With a weak smile, she looked Kenny over. He was out cold. She could reach him. She just had to stretch. With a shaking hand, Izzy started searching his pockets. Just as her hand closed over the pocket knife, secured in the pocket of his jacket, Kenny started to snore. Izzy felt the knife slip from her fingers as the sound startled her. "I can do this," she whispered.

"You're really brave, Miss Izzy. You're the bravest librarian I've ever seen," Billy hung over the seat, watching her every movement.

"Thanks." Izzy didn't feel brave. She slowly went for the knife again. "Got it!" She held it for Billy's inspection. Izzy opened the door. They both frowned. The car's dome light shone on a blade that looked dull.

The snow blew into the car like an infestation of tiny white specks. Izzy tried to ignore the cold, but her hands shook. It took over fifteen minutes to cut the rope. Hot chocolate, her mother's quilt, and a roaring fire, that's what she wanted. Staying here would not get it. "Come on, Billy."

"My pants are wet."

"Grab another pair out of the pillowcase." Izzy rubbed her hands together, surprised that she could think rationally enough to remember that they'd brought extra clothes.

Billy changed his pants faster than she'd ever seen a child dress. While he dressed, she opened the glove compartment and grabbed her flashlight. He climbed over the seat and together they crawled out of the car.

"Your hand looks really bad," Billy observed.

"It will be okay. Come on, Buster." She adopted Parker's pet word, hoping it would help keep Billy's spirits up.

Her tennis shoes sank into what felt like slushy ice. The snow brushed under her pant leg. Izzy took a deep breath as the cold melted around her sock, pricking against her ankle like tiny knives. Tears of frustration started in her eyes. God had gotten them out of the frying pan, but there was still the fire to contend with. The flashlight seemed inadequate against the weather. It's beam didn't seem able to penetrate the darkness.

"Are you crying?" Billy wanted to know.

"It's been a bad day." Izzy tried to sound casual.

" 'A very bad, rotten, no-good day.' " Billy recited from a book Izzy had read aloud to him the weekend she'd baby-sat.

They were both miserable before they reached the side of the interstate. Izzy held tightly to Billy's hand, wondering if they should attempt to make it back to the rest stop, or if they should try to flag down a motorist. In this weather they were more likely to be run over than noticed.

"Do you like to sing, Billy?"

"Ah-ha."

Izzy had just started "Jesus Loves Me" when a bright pair of headlights penetrated the swirling snow. Izzy tugged on Billy's hand and ran toward the road. Miraculously, the truck pulled off to the side. Izzy blinked away the snowflakes that were threatening to blind her and stumbled toward the vehicle. The driver's-side door opened, and Izzy could just make out the dome light inside. One driver and a dog. No! Izzy squinted. One Parker and a Brute! Izzy started to run, but

Parker was already there grabbing her into his warm arms and picking up Billy.

"I found you." He blanketed her in his arms. For a frozen moment, his unshaven chin gently scratched against her face. "I prayed. For the first time in years, I prayed."

"Parker," she whispered. "I can't believe you could see us in this weather."

Even with Billy clutched to him, Parker's lips closed over hers and suddenly, for a brief second, she wasn't cold.

The weather couldn't be ignored for long, and as she began to shake, she managed to say, "How did you find us?"

He took the flashlight from her hand. "I'd say that this is powered by more than batteries. I saw the light plainly. It was like a beacon."

She shivered, not just from the cold. "Kenny's back there. He might be hurt. And, Parker, he has a gun."

Parker helped them into the truck and tucked a blanket securely around their shivering forms. He climbed in and quickly radioed his location and stated that he would check out the situation and then attempt to get any injured party to Grand Island. Brute excitedly washed the wet snow from Billy's face, only making the boy shiver.

"I'm leaving the heater on. I'm going to go get Kenny. I doubt if he's hurt. His body was probably too relaxed from the alcohol to feel any pain. You didn't hit anything did you?"

"No, we just went a little ways into the ditch."

"I was scared," Billy said. "But Izzy said it didn't matter because she was scared, too, and that there was an angel in the car with us. I didn't see him. I tried not be scared. I told God to send Grandpa after us, but it's okay that He sent you."

"Well," Parker said slowly, "I'm glad it's okay. After the kind of day you've had," Parker tousled Billy's hair, "you'll be known as the bravest boy around. I'm sure proud of you for taking care of Izzy."

The moment Parker slammed the door and walked away, the truck lost its security. Billy's eyes had been gleaming proudly while Parker praised him, but now he snuggled closer to Izzy and buried his head in her side. Brute put a paw on Billy's leg and rested his head against the boy.

Billy stared out the window for a moment, then asked, "Why did Kenny take us? What was he going to do?"

Izzy stroked Billy's hair, allowing her hand to pass briefly over his forehead. He still felt warm. Poor little tyke. Three weeks ago his biggest obstacle had been conquering the old elm in the library's park; now he'd been separated from his mother, found out he had the world's worst father, run away, been kidnapped, and all this before he'd even lost his first tooth.

"Kenny took us because he wanted attention," Izzy said.

"What?" Billy sat up.

"Remember how you yelled at Parker that you wanted to go see your mother?"

Billy nodded.

"You wanted his attention, so you yelled. Kenny likes to yell, too, only he does it while drinking. When he took us, he was yelling for attention."

Billy didn't look convinced, but he was listening.

"And remember how you ran away to go looking for your mother?"

Billy smiled proudly.

"Kenny was running away, taking us with him, because he needed help and didn't think anyone was listening."

"I guess he doesn't know that God will listen," Billy said thoughtfully.

twelve

Parker came back carrying Kenny over his shoulder, as if his cousin weighed no more than a sack of flour. With sudden insight, Izzy realized that rescuing Kenny came naturally to Parker. He'd probably been doing it since childhood. Another reason Parker made such a good fireman.

"Will Billy be okay if I put Kenny inside?" Parker tried to duck down enough to look at Billy's face. Kenny's head banged against the top of the truck. Kenny moaned but didn't wake up.

Izzy tilted Billy's head up and caressed his forehead. With the innocence of a child, Billy slumbered peacefully, looking as if the day had been typical. Brute lay in the boy's lap, a sleeping watchpuppy. No sign of stress creased Billy's brow.

"If we're careful, Billy won't even know." Gently, Izzy scooted Billy over so that he was near the steering wheel.

Parked loaded Kenny into the extended cab. Brute whined and rearranged his position.

"I'll hurry," Parker promised, getting in the truck and seeing the worry in Izzy's face as she brushed Billy's bangs out of his eyes. Then he glanced at the thickness of night that waited on the deserted interstate. "But it will be a slow hurry."

They continued on toward Kearney before finding an emergency cutoff that allowed them to turn around and head the opposite way. Parker didn't talk. He hunched forward, looking as if he was cradling the steering wheel as he tried to make out the road before him.

"Do you think my car's all right?" Izzy couldn't take the silence anymore.

"No, we're going to get you a new one. A truck." Parker gripped the steering wheel tighter.

"I don't want a truck. I like my car. We just slid into a ditch. I know it will have a little front-end damage, but surely it can be fixed."

"If we fix it, you can only drive it in summer. You'll need a truck for winters."

"Parker, what are you talking about? Why will I need a truck for winters? Plus, if I get a new vehicle I'm quite capable of choosing my own. I chose the Peugeot."

Briefly, Parker took his eyes away from the road. "Yes, that's obvious."

"Are you mad at me?" Izzy whispered with a huff. "The accident wasn't my fault. What is this, 'We'll get a new car? You can only drive in summer.' This morning—"

Parker hit the brakes, maintaining perfect control of the truck as he swerved over to the emergency lane and braked. "I was trying to make it to Grand Island before I did this. I don't want Billy to wake up and see Kenny, but. . . ."

Without another word, Parker pulled Izzy to him, planting a firm kiss on her lips, which warmed her all the way to her toes. His cold fingers came up to caress her cheeks as he took possession of her mouth.

"Parker," she murmured.

He tore his lips away. "I love you, Isobelle de la Rosa. When I found out that Kenny had taken you, I imagined that little car of yours against a tree and your pretty face sheet white, and—" Parker stopped. "I prayed, Izzy. And He answered. You were right all along. I couldn't have found you without His help. Still, I never want to worry about such a thing again. When we're married, if you want to go to Lincoln to shop, I'll take you. But if you need to get around town, it's going to be in a four-wheel drive, painted cherry red, so that if you ever go off the road I can find you."

"Married? Married!" Numbly, Izzy repeated the word as she tried to savor the warmth that marked the place his lips had been a moment earlier. Here it was, her first proposal that she might accept—and she sat in the front seat of a truck, holding a little boy while a madman slumbered behind her. "Parker, are you proposing?"

He kissed her again, quickly, tenderly, holding one hand behind her head. Brute whimpered. Parker pulled away, looking at her, and then took his foot off the brake, giving his attention to the white road ahead. Slowly, the truck began the tedious crawl back on the interstate. As they pulled off the Grand Island exit, the grayness lifted a bit, and Izzy saw a piece of morning white sky. Another night spent in chaotic adventure. Things were looking better, even for a Monday.

"Yes, I'm proposing. Are you going to answer?" Parker asked.

"I'm cold."

"Besides that."

"I'm hungry." This should be a moment of gladness, but fatigue nestled deep. Marriage to Parker? She could imagine that. But, was he ready? Had he comes to terms with man and God? He was pretty excited about finding her and quite willing to give credit to God. But what about later, when he had time to think?

A flashing red and white beam highlighted the truck's cab. Izzy glanced at the side mirror and said a little prayer of thanks that a cruiser had them in sight. Parker pulled over into the parking lot of a fast food restaurant. Another cruiser joined the first and pulled in behind them.

Izzy stayed in the truck, holding Billy. She watched as Parker animatedly spoke with the police officers. After a few minutes they came and pulled Kenny out of the cab. Two cops shook their heads and lifted him between them to walk back to their cruiser.

Parker got behind the wheel. "We have to follow them to the station. You need to fill out a complaint; not that they intend to hold him just for kidnapping."

"I almost feel sorry for him," Izzy said.

"I used to, but after the scare he gave me today, I'm through picking up after him."

Parker parked the truck on the street in front of the Grand Island Police Station. Billy scrambled out of the truck, a bit woozy. He let Parker carry him inside. The station lobby had hard, green plastic chairs pressed against olive-colored walls reminiscent of the sixties, with dark forest tile underfoot. Izzy took Billy on her lap while Parker went to the pay phone to call his mother.

Billy looked around. "What's going on?"

"We're at the police station in Grand Island. They arrested Kenny, and we have to tell them what happened."

"Will we get to go home then?"

"I don't know." Izzy looked outside. Snow pelted against the door panes, making Izzy feel as if she were trapped inside one of those snow-scene paperweight decorations. Water globes, that's what they were called. But she could not recall one that had a jailhouse for setting.

Parker left the pay phone and walked to the counter. Two women were busy typing at desks. He cleared his throat and leaned over to ask them something. Izzy couldn't make out his words, but the answer seemed to annoy him. She watched as he flipped out his identification and tapped his finger impatiently on the counter. One of the women picked up a phone and dialed. After a moment she relayed some information to Parker, who shook his head in irritation before walking back to Izzy.

"They're really backed up." Parker shook his head. "She's calling the captain now, but it looks as if we'll need to take a room at one of the local motels and wait until a more reasonable hour to give them your statement."

"Do you think there are any rooms available? We saw lots of cars pulling into motels when Kenny got gas earlier."

"The local police keep a motel room on retainer, just in case." Parker didn't explain the "just in case" and Izzy immediately fantasized about Texas Rangers transporting criminals back to the state line or hostile witnesses held against their will until trial date.

An elevator door opened. So enthralled with her meanderings, Izzy hadn't even noticed that there was an elevator. A tall, brown-haired man with dark circles under his eyes stepped out. He walked over and shook Parker's hand, nodding at Izzy.

"I just got off the phone with—" he checked a small notebook, "an Officer ·Rowe. He gave me everything I need to book Kenny Latkam. We still want a statement from you Miss de la Rosa, but that can wait until later. We've arranged for a room at the Holiday Inn. Do you know where that is?"

Parker nodded, leaning over and pulling Izzy up.

"Unfortunately, due to the weather, they've only got the one room. It has two double beds. Will that be a problem?" The captain looked at Izzy, and then Parker, as if imagining a binding between them.

"No," Parker said. "As long as they don't mind my dog. He's in the truck. We're tired. We just want to sleep. Thanks for postponing the report until tomorrow."

"Yes, that is a problem," interrupted Izzy. "Parker, I'm sorry. I trust you and all that, but. . ."

The captain nodded. "Let me make a call. There's a fire station just down the road. What with you being a fireman, I'm sure they'll let you bunk there for the rest of the night. Here's my card. Get something to eat and give me a ring."

Parker took Billy from Izzy and they went back to his truck to head for the Holiday Inn. He had stayed here twice before. Both times he'd testified concerning criminals wanted by both Mayhill and Grand Island police. He pulled in a reserved spot by the front door and lifted Billy out of the truck. The "No Vacancy" sign blinked orange and off.

❧

Snow crunched underfoot as Izzy followed Parker inside. Objecting to sharing the room had come automatically. The words had, that is. She knew her beliefs. Unfortunately, her imagination longed for something else. Still, telling him she wouldn't share a room with him, even platonically, and with

Billy as a chaperone, sent him a message. He knew where he stood. Where she stood. Even her overactive imagination knew what Jesus would do.

Billy perked up the moment Parker opened the door to their room.

"I want down. This is great. Just wait until show-and-tell at school. I've never stayed in a motel before. Can I sleep in the bed by the window? Can we turn the television on?" Billy jumped from one location to another with Brute at his heels. Before Izzy or Parker could answer his questions, he peeled his coat off and tried to take a hanger down from the closet. "Hey! These hangers are broken. This one won't come down."

Parker hung up Billy's coat.

Billy ducked under his arm and went to jump on the bed. Brute followed, letting out a loud woof, and trying to keep up with Billy. The coarse orange and brown bedspread slid to the side.

"Billy, stop. People are trying to sleep."

As if a puppeteer had cut the strings, Billy settled on the bed. Brute ran back to Parker, then returned to Billy.

"It's been quite a day—er, night." Izzy straightened the bedspread. "He's wide awake now." She watched as Billy investigated under the bed. Checking her watch, she said, "Parker, it's almost five in the morning. I don't know whether to put Billy to sleep, or feed him breakfast. It's going to take a while for him to wind down."

"Do you want to go down to the restaurant and get something to eat, or shall I go over to McDonald's and pick something up?" Parker hesitated in taking off his coat.

"I'd rather eat in the restaurant. That okay with you, Billy?" She felt his forehead. He felt fine. Amazing.

"Restaurant! Sure. Do they have spaghetti?"

Poor kid, who knew when he'd get his internal clock adjusted? Spaghetti for breakfast? Truthfully, Izzy thought as she went into the rest room, Billy had been so brave, he deserved whatever he wanted. She looked in the mirror.

Splashing cold water on her face, she tried to wipe some of the grime off. "Parker! Maybe we should eat in. I look terrible."

Parker's face suddenly joined hers in the mirror. He stood inches taller than she, and the effect looked like a studio portrait. "I think you look beautiful. You didn't answer my question about getting married." Parker stepped closer, propping one hand against the bathroom wall.

Izzy ducked under Parker's arm. "I think going out to eat is just the thing for Billy. You need to talk to him about Kenny, explain that your cousin is sick."

"I'll do that." Parker looked thoughtful. "You don't think Billy's going to need counseling or anything, do you?"

"Not with all the attention your family is going to give him when we get back."

"And his new cousin?"

"I'm hungry." Izzy poked him in the ribs. "Put Brute in the rest room and let's go."

The Holiday Inn restaurant was just opening for breakfast. A hostess informed them it would be a few minutes. Billy went down to his knees by a basket of giveaway toys. Parker sat down next to Izzy on the vinyl bench and put his arm comfortably about her shoulders.

"Do you know how scared I was when I figured out that Kenny had your car, with you and Billy in it?" Parker took her hand.

"Not nearly as scared as I was." Izzy leaned back, closing her eyes, enjoying the feeling of Parker toying with the sensitive skin of her palm.

"That's true. Why did you go down into the cellar?"

"I wanted to do your laundry."

"My laundry?" Parker gave her a funny look. "Whatever for?"

"Billy had spilled his soup. I wanted clean clothes for him, and I wanted to get the house in order so that nothing would distract me when you finally came home. I needed to talk to you."

"You didn't need to do my laundry."

"I know I didn't need to. I wanted to."

"What did you so desperately intend to tell me this morning?"

"I wanted to explain my actions. Parker, do you remember when you returned all those library books?"

"How could I forget? Kenny's library fine cost a month's worth of groceries."

"When you turned the books in, I didn't realize they were Kenny's."

Parker shrugged. "So you were upset at me for having massive library fines?"

"No!" Izzy disentangled her arm and turned to face him. "Remember how I chased you down and handed you back one of the books?"

"I remember."

"Did you look to see what that book was?"

"No. It belonged to Kenny. It was private."

"You're right. It was Kenny's journal. I opened it to see if there was a name, but there wasn't. I read the first paragraph by accident. It was all about suicide. I thought it was yours."

"You thought it was mine? Why?"

"I'd never seen Kenny's handwriting. I'd never even seen him in the library. You were returning the books. You paid the fine, and you were so sad. I just assumed it was yours."

"So you started pestering me because you thought I might kill myself?"

"Yes."

Parker pulled her closer to him and put his arm around her again. "I think that's sweet."

"You're not mad?"

"Of course not. I was worried that you were afraid of relationships, because of what your father had done. Now that I know you thought I had some of the same emotional problems that your father did, I can see why you were so skittish. Since we have all this out of the way, are you going to marry me?"

"Strickland," the hostess said over a microphone. It sounded unusually loud against the silence of the restaurant.

Billy ran up with a fistful of plastic toys.

"He can only take one," the hostess said.

Izzy whispered to the hostess. "He's had a really bad day."

"Yes, but—"

" 'A really bad, rotten, no-good day,' " Izzy repeated.

"I read that book." The hostess smiled as she led them to a corner booth.

❧

Izzy had crawled into the bed by the door. Billy took the one by the window. After a few minutes of horseplay, he settled down. Izzy's eyes were closing when Billy started complaining that he couldn't sleep with the outside light throwing its glare at him. They changed beds. Now, the feeble glow from the flickering motel sign shone on Izzy. She was no longer tired, and thoughts of Kenny and Parker played over and over in her mind. Breakfast had ended too quickly. The need to get a drooping Billy into bed had stalled Parker from attempting any more marriage proposals. Izzy wondered what Parker was thinking about.

She'd wanted him to propose! Only not in twenty-degree weather with his cousin passed out in the extended cab. He hadn't mentioned Julia, either. Just when had he decided to chance marriage again? He'd been so distant that day in the library. An unsmiling man with a chip on his shoulder. The suddenness of his change in disposition unsettled Izzy. Could he have found peace that quickly? And what kind of peace had he found? It was too much, too new. Maybe she could have the preacher. . .

A fierce knocking woke her up. Stumbling, she wrapped the blanket around her and went to the door. "Wake up!" Parker stood there, offering chocolate doughnuts and a carton of milk.

Izzy cleared her throat. "What time is it?"

"Half past three. You've been asleep for over seven hours."

"Have you checked the weather?"

"Yes. It's stopped snowing. The Grand Island police are waiting for us, and Billy needs to get home so we can find out about his mother. I tried calling the hospital, but no one answered the phone in Delta's room. My folks aren't home and neither are the McKennas."

"Give us a minute."

"I'll take Brute for a walk and meet you in the lobby."

Not even as a child had Izzy liked putting on the same clothes twice. "First thing I'm going to do when I get home is take a shower," she yelled at Billy from the bathroom.

"You look fine," Billy said, sounding much like an adult.

Once they were downstairs, Parker backed up Billy's words. Standing up to greet them, he touched her hair and said, "You're the best-looking woman here."

"You know," Izzy said, giving Parker a long look, "you just might have possibilities."

"Does that mean you'll marry me?"

"That means I'll allow you to buy me a diet soda from that machine over there."

Parker saluted before walking to the machine.

"If you marry Parker," Billy said, "can I still come over and eat peanut butter jelly sandwiches for breakfast. . .?" Billy took a deep breath, and Izzy had a feeling the best part was coming. "And not clean up afterwards?" Billy finished.

Parker handed her a cold soda and answered for her. "If Izzy marries me you can come over in the morning and have pop-tarts. That's what Izzy eats. Right Izzy?" He opened the door of the motel and ushered them out.

"How do you know?"

"Whip. He's real concerned that you didn't cook much." Parker opened the truck door for her.

"He's always cooking." Izzy didn't like the disbelief on his face. "Parker, I can cook. Ask my mother. Ask Fred Rasmussen. Ask Mark Dalton." She listed everyone she could think of as they got in the truck.

Parker frowned when she mentioned Mark Dalton's name.

"I don't care if you can't cook. I'm a good cook. Most firemen are." He started the engine, waiting a moment for the truck to warm up.

"He makes great peanut butter and jelly sandwiches," Billy agreed.

The brick police station seemed a more friendly place without the swirling, night snow as a background. They rolled the window down just a bit, wrapped Brute in a blanket—which he promptly shook off—and went inside. The same brown-haired captain greeted them from the elevator, and rode with them down to a tiny office. He sat behind an ancient wooden desk and handed Izzy three blue information sheets to fill out. Parker watched over her shoulder as she filled in the personal data.

The captain cleared his throat. "Your cousin's in the holding cell. If you want to see him, I've told the duty officer to let you in. It might be a while before he's transported back to Mayhill."

Parker nodded. "I'd appreciate that."

With Parker gone, it was easier to tell the captain about Kenny's behavior. Billy sat, all grown-up like, in the wooden chair next to Izzy and nodded at her words. The interview didn't take long. To Izzy's surprise, the captain was more interested in the information she'd written down than in what she told him. The last thing he did was hand her a white card that had his phone number on it and a report number.

"If you remember anything else, Miss de la Rosa, contact me." His beeper sounded and he nodded that she could leave.

Parker paced the waiting room. "Let's go."

Silently, Parker helped Izzy and Billy into the truck, his actions making it clear that he didn't feel like conversation. They left Grand Island with the distant October sun laughing down at the feeble attempt of the snow to remain a blanket. Slush flew from both sides of the truck as Parker headed for Mayhill.

"Parker, what happened?" Izzy shed her coat.

"He thought I was there to bail him out."

"Doesn't he know how much trouble he's in?"

"I don't think he does." Parker shook his head and repeated sadly, "He really thought I was there to bail him out." They drove the rest of the way home with the radio tuned to a country station focusing on heartbreak songs.

Officer Rowe waited, sitting inside his patrol car, in front of Izzy's apartment. Parker had barely stopped the car and hopped out to shake the man's hand before Francine screeched to a halt and ran toward Billy.

"Edna's at our house. I think she's having a nervous breakdown. Delta's doing fine." Francine's hand shook as she pulled Billy into her arms. "Mr. and Mrs. McKenna got home last night. I filled them in on all that's been happening."

"Grandpa?" Billy grinned. "Can I go home now?"

"Why don't you take him, Parker? I need to ask Izzy a few questions, and your mother's beat." Officer Rowe reached for the pen in his shirt pocket.

Parker looked ready to argue, but then he looked at his mother. "Izzy, is it—?"

"Go ahead, Parker. I'll be fine."

Whip came out of the house and wandered down to the conversation. "Catherine's doing fine. She's called twice and told me to tell you to take the day off. I think she's enjoying coming out of retirement."

Officer Rowe nodded. "I did stop by the library this morning on the off chance that you'd returned last night, and I'd missed you. She was mumbling something about only the coffeemaker being worth keeping and that libraries need books, not computers."

"Will you be okay, Izzy?" Parker held Billy's hand.

"I'll be fine." Izzy started to follow Officer Rowe into the house. She paused at the front door.

Parker stopped to talk to his mother. Izzy went back to the porch, sat in the rocker, and watched them. The cold seeped through her coat.

"Hurry up, Parker!" Billy climbed in the truck and hugged Brute.

"Just a minute." Parker left his mother and walked back to the porch.

"I've got some cream to go with that coffee, just inside." Whip motioned at Officer Rowe.

"I don't use cream."

"Today's a good day to start," Whip recommended, giving Officer Rowe a look of elderly authority that the policeman decided to obey.

Parker's mother drove off.

"Izzy," Parker said stepping onto the porch, "will you marry me?"

"Hmmm," Izzy said, folding her hands in front of her.

Parker got down on one knee. "Will you marry me?"

"This is happening so fast." Izzy tried to smile. He looked so handsome. She wanted to freeze the moment and sit down and admire him. It wasn't just his looks. It was a strength he had, both physically and mentally. She touched his hair and thought that although she'd just been through a terrifying couple of days she had never been happier. She squatted down and looked into his eyes. "You know how little girls dream about the man they're going to marry, write their names in the margin of notebooks, and wonder how many children they might have?"

"Somewhat," Parker acknowledged, helping her up.

"I always did that, but there was one other thing. Parker, there's not supposed to be just two in a marriage."

"What do you mean?"

"I mean, I only believe a marriage can work if God is the third member of the union."

"Now you're going a little fast. I can promise I'll think about it." Parker reached out, gently took her hand, and brushed his lips against her knuckles.

"Okay," Izzy said, "then I can promise I'll think about it too."

Parker raised one eyebrow. "For how long?"

"As long as it takes you."

thirteen

The white dress trailed two inches onto the floor.

"Rosemary was taller than you," Francine said, the pins in her mouth moving up and down with each word. The Strickland living room looked as if a fabric-store tornado had descended.

"I'm not sure I should wear this for the centennial." Izzy studied her reflection in a handheld mirror, fingered the ancient lace around her neck, and fidgeted.

"If you're changing your mind again, you get to tell Jake." Carole bounced seven-month-old Jessica Kayla Martin up and down on her knee and cooed.

"This dress belongs in a museum," Izzy argued. "What if I spill something on it?"

"Rosemary already did," Francine said, fingering a yellowing spot near Izzy's knee. "I hope I can get that out without the material tearing. I can't believe you found this dress. I'd forgotten about that old hope chest."

Clara Bryant handed Francine the measuring tape. "That dress looks like it was made for you."

"Mom." Izzy rolled her eyes.

"She's right," Francine agreed. "I couldn't have squeezed into this bridal gown on my wedding day if I tried. You're the perfect choice to reenact the highlights of Rosemary Mayhill. What a coincidence you noticed that Rosemary's wedding day happened to fall on the same day as the centennial. We're thrilled to have you join our family." Francine smiled warmly at Clara. "I can hardly wait for Thanksgiving. Just imagine all of us around the dinner table."

"I don't know if I can do this." Izzy fingered the white lace that clung against her arm.

Walking backwards, Edna butted the screen door open and let everyone know she had been eavesdropping. "Sure you can. Isobelle, you're going to make a sensational bride. I can't believe it was just seven months ago you were going to leave." Edna laughed, watching Izzy turn red. "I heartily approve of Parker's choice for a wife. Where is he?"

"He took one look at his mother, armed with her sewing basket, and mumbled something about the garden and fertilizer." Izzy rolled her eyes. Parker hadn't wanted a big production for his wedding, but after Mayor Martin visited the library and mentioned to Izzy how nice a separate information desk would look next to the biography section, Parker knew he'd be getting married the old-fashioned way, complete with homespun trousers and suspenders.

"I went through mother's jewelry and found this." Edna held out a silver locket. "And look." Edna waved a curled, old black and white photograph in front of them. It showed Rosemary and Darby Mayhill. "See." Edna puffed, exasperated that she had to point out the minute details. "The necklace. She's wearing it."

"That's fantastic," Carole admired the picture. "Izzy, do you have everything you need for Saturday night?"

"I can't believe I let Jake talk us into getting married the evening of the centennial. There's so much going on." Butterflies hit Izzy's stomach with the force of an air force squadron.

"It's perfect," Francine said, "especially since the Wilfongs are letting Parker borrow their old buggy."

Izzy closed her eyes and tried to remember how she'd reverted from being a single woman whose greatest concern was that her cat liked liver and became, not a blushing contemporary bride, but an imitation turn-of-the-century bride.

"This dress can count as the something old." Francine finished pinning.

Carole added, "The veil is new."

"You've got something borrowed," Edna said, holding up the necklace.

"And I'll lend you something blue." Delta came in dragging a reluctant Billy along.

"I don't want to come in," Billy protested. "I want to go in the backyard and play with Parker and Brute."

"It will only take me a moment to pin his pants." Francine stepped back, releasing Izzy from scrutiny.

"Billy," Izzy said. "I really do appreciate you being our ring bearer."

"Aw, that's all right."

Edna took Billy under the shoulders and stood him on the stool Izzy had just vacated.

"You'll be the best ring bearer ever," Edna bragged.

"Mama, I gotta. . ." Billy squirmed.

"Go ahead," Delta urged.

Billy scampered down the hall.

"He's still having trouble sleeping. Doctor Taylor says he'll get over it. Other than that, he seems to have forgotten all about that day."

The women all nodded solemnly.

"Kenny's doing better," Edna defended her son. "Whip's been visiting him at the prison and seems to think Kenny figured out that it's time to grow up."

"That's wonderful." Francine hugged her sister. "We've been attending a Bible study with Whip, too. You ought to come, Edna." Francine giggled. "Do you remember when Rosemary would take us to church on Sundays? We'd be dressed in our Sunday best and afraid to move. I didn't realize how much I missed it. Worse, I don't even remember when we stopped going. We missed a Sunday, then another Sunday, and suddenly we didn't even think of attending church. Between Whip, Izzy, and Parker, it looks as if the Lord is showing us where we belong."

Izzy smiled and looked at her reflection in the mirror. In just two days, she would would be Isobelle Strickland. In the last seven months, she had watched Parker go from a questioning man sitting in a Bible study to a devout man convincing others of his newfound love. Jesus first, yourself last, and others in between. He took joy in his new freedom. He had written a letter to Julia's parents and sent them some of her belongings. His thirst for scriptural knowledge had overflowed and caught Izzy in the current. His life gave evidence of Ephesians 5:14: "Wake up, O sleeper, rise from the dead, and Christ will shine on you." Parker had been baptized just one month after proposing to Izzy for the first time. Since then, nothing had stopped his spiritual growth.

"A, B, C. . ." Billy's singsong voice echoed down the hall.

"I got his report card," Delta bragged. "Guess what subject his first grade teacher commended him in."

"Music," Carole shouted, only a breath ahead of Francine and Edna.

"As a librarian," Izzy scolded Carole, "you should have said 'reading.' "

৯

Mayor Martin sat, not in the front row, but in the second row. His neck, wrinkling like a turkey's, turned every thirty seconds while he scanned the aisle, anxiously waiting for Izzy to appear in the back door.

Parker waited by the preacher. Every time Jake Martin turned his head, Parker plucked at the bow tie collar that was choking him. Next to Parker stood Robert Parrish, Ty Horner, and Jeff Henly, all looking equally uncomfortable in their turn-of-the-century-groomsmen outfits.

A hum carried over the church. Parker scanned the audience, amazed to see that every pew was packed, and that with nowhere else available to sit, people were standing against the wall.

"What do you think is keeping her?" Jake whispered to Carole.

Parker strained to hear Carole's answer. If she had one, he wanted to know too.

"It takes a woman a while to get ready for her wedding. Especially if she's wearing an heirloom bridal gown."

"She did a great job acting like Rosemary today." For a moment, Jake relaxed.

Carole fixed Jake with a stern look. "With Parker at her side, she felt very much like a part of Rosemary's family. I can't believe you made her wear a 'Vote for Martin' pin."

Jake squirmed. "It didn't look so bad. Did you notice her saying some things during her speech that weren't in her research?"

The baby hiccuped. Carole cradled Jessica against her shoulder and nodded. "I noticed that, too. I wonder where she located more information. I had no idea that Rosemary was three years older than Darby."

The church's hum grew louder. Jake looked back and nudged Carole. "There she is."

Every head turned. Parker stood straighter. Izzy's skirt occupied almost the entire doorway. Billy and the little Summer girl waited for the nod from Francine that meant they should walk. Parker swallowed. Izzy had never looked more beautiful than tonight. And the lion's share of her beauty was inside. She'd given him so much: love, commitment, and the Lord.

Izzy gave Billy a gentle push. Billy took a few steps and then hurried back to Izzy. The little boy tugged on the lace sleeve of Izzy's bridal gown. Parker watched as Izzy listened for a moment and then nodded. Billy disappeared out the door.

"What's going on?" Jake Martin's hiss brought disapproving stares.

Over the heads of the witnesses, Izzy's eyes met Parker's. I love you, she mouthed.

I love you, too, he mouthed back.

His collar stopped choking. The organist hit one note, stopped, and leaned forward to listen. The entire church followed the woman's example.

"A, B, C, D. . ." Billy McKenna's singsong voice, at a distance, entertained the guests at Parker and Izzy's wedding.

A Letter To Our Readers

Dear Reader:

In order that we might better contribute to your reading enjoyment, we would appreciate your taking a few minutes to respond to the following questions. We welcome your comments and read each form and letter we receive. When completed, please return to the following:

Rebecca Germany, Fiction Editor
Heartsong Presents
PO Box 719
Uhrichsville, Ohio 44683

1. Did you enjoy reading *It Only Takes a Spark?*
   ☐ Very much. I would like to see more books
      by this author!
   ☐ Moderately
      I would have enjoyed it more if _____

      _____

      _____

2. Are you a member of **Heartsong Presents**? Yes ☐ No ☐
   If no, where did you purchase this book? _____

   _____

3. How would you rate, on a scale from 1 (poor) to 5 (superior),
   the cover design? _____

4. On a scale from 1 (poor) to 10 (superior), please rate the
   following elements.

   _____ Heroine   _____ Plot

   _____ Hero   _____ Inspirational theme

   _____ Setting   _____ Secondary characters

5. These characters were special because_____

_____

_____

6. How has this book inspired your life?_____

_____

_____

7. What settings would you like to see covered in future **Heartsong Presents** books?_____

_____

_____

8. What are some inspirational themes you would like to see treated in future books?_____

_____

_____

9. Would you be interested in reading other **Heartsong Presents** titles?   Yes ☐   No ☐

10. Please check your age range:
    ☐ Under 18   ☐ 18-24   ☐ 25-34
    ☐ 35-45   ☐ 46-55   ☐ Over 55

11. How many hours per week do you read?_____

Name _____

Occupation _____

Address _____

City _____ State _____ Zip _____

Daily inspiration for Women

The apostle Peter wrote that a gentle spirit, not our outward appearance, is of great worth in God's sight. In our harsh and often heartless world, gentleness is a much-needed characteristic. With an emphasis on personal spiritual development, this daily devotional for women draws from the best writings of classic and contemporary Christian female authors.

384 pages, Printed Leatherette, 4 ³/₁₆" x 6 ³/₄"

❤ ❤ ❤ ❤ ❤ ❤ ❤ ❤ ❤ ♥ ❤ ❤ ❤ ❤ ❤ ❤ ❤

Please send me _____ copies of *A Gentle Spirit*. I am enclosing $4.97 each. (Please add $1.00 to cover postage and handling per order. OH add 6% tax.)

Send check or money order, no cash or C.O.D.s please.

Name_____

Address _____

City, State, Zip _____

To place a credit card order, call 1-800-847-8270.

Send to: Heartsong Presents Reader Service, PO Box 719, Uhrichsville, OH 44683

❤ ❤ ❤ ❤ ❤ ❤ ❤ ❤ ♥ ❤ ❤ ❤ ❤ ❤ ❤ ❤ ❤

MB.*

Heartsong Presents
Love Stories
Are Rated G!

That's for godly, gratifying, and of course, great! If you love a
thrilling love story, but don't appreciate the sordidness of some
popular paperback romances, **Heartsong Presents** is for you. In
fact, **Heartsong Presents** is the *only inspirational romance book
club*, the only one featuring love stories where Christian faith is
the primary ingredient in a marriage relationship.

Sign up today to receive your first set of four, never before
published Christian romances. Send no money now; you will
receive a bill with the first shipment. You may cancel at any time
without obligation, and if you aren't completely satisfied with
any selection, you may return the books for an immediate refund!

Imagine. . .four new romances every four weeks—two historical, two contemporary—with men and women like you who
long to meet the one God has chosen as the love of their lives. .
.all for the low price of $9.97 postpaid.

*To join, simply complete the coupon below and mail to the
address provided.* **Heartsong Presents** romances are rated G for
another reason: They'll arrive *Godspeed!*